RESERVOIR OF SECRETS

RESERVOIR OF SECRETS

PARKS PAT MYSTERIES
BOOK FOURTEEN

P.D. WORKMAN

PD WORKMAN

ISBN: 9781774688496 (KDP Paperback)
ISBN: 9781774688502 (KDP Hardcover)
ISBN: 9781774688526 (Lulu Paperback)
ISBN: 9781774688519 (Large Print)
ISBN: 9781774688533 (Digital)
ISBN: 9781774688540 (Auto-narrated audiobook)

ALSO BY P.D. WORKMAN

MYSTERY/SUSPENSE:

Parks Pat Mysteries
Police Procedural Set in Canada
Out with the Sunset
Long Climb to the Top
Dark Water Under the Bridge
Immersed in the View
Skimming Over the Lake
Hazard of the Hills
Knows the Hills
Spanning the Creek
Sanctuary in the Stream
Echoes of the Engine
Bench with a View
Beneath the Icy Depths
Grounded in the Wind (Coming Soon)
Reservoir of Secrets (Coming Soon)
Peril in the Blooms (Coming Soon)

Kenzie Kirsch Medical Thrillers
Unlawful Harvest
Doctored Death
Dosed to Death

Gentle Angel

Rushin' Death

Posed for Death

Death of a Corpse

Endowed with Death

Shattered to Death

Captured in Death

Currying Death

Healed to Death

Death's Charm

Bleeding Hearts Valley Thrillers
An Abrupt Departure

High-Tech Crime Solvers Series
Virtually Harmless

Cowritten with D. D. VanDyke
California Corwin P. I. Mystery Series
The Girl in the Morgue

Stand Alone Suspense Novels
Looking Over Your Shoulder

Lion Within

Pursued by the Past

In the Tick of Time

Loose the Dogs

AND MORE AT PDWORKMAN.COM

For patriarchs and matriarchs
who gather family in

STYLE NOTE

Since my largest readership is in the USA, I have chosen to use US spellings throughout this series. That includes the Americanization of centre to center, even where it is an actual place name, just for consistency's sake. I apologize to my Canadian readers for this.

I have chosen, however, to use Canadian grammar, particularly for Canadian voices. If you see what you think is a grammar error, it may just be Canadian, eh?

CHAPTER ONE

*I*t was the perfect day for a picnic in Glenmore Park. Margie was glad it had warmed up and they could get in their first real outing of the year. Moushoom needed a sweater to keep his old body warm, but the rest of them were in shirt sleeves, enjoying the freedom from coats and mittens and other winter gear. Christina's brown face glowed in the sunlight. She looked happy and carefree, as if school and its accompanying stresses were distant memories. A gentle breeze blew over the reservoir and fluttered the bright green leaves of the trees.

It should have been the perfect day, unfolding just as Margie had planned.

It wasn't even like it was a big family get-together. She and Christina wanted to get the extended family together and have a big gathering of the cousins, but they were starting small, with just their little family, and would work on planning something bigger in the summer, getting everyone organized. Like the family at the picnic area next to theirs. Three generations with a vigorous-looking patriarch at their head. Maybe in his seventies, considering the ages of his children, he looked like he could have challenged any of the other adults there or even the grandchildren to a sports challenge. Running, swimming, weightlifting. She didn't know what his sport was, but it was clear that he followed some kind of regimen to keep himself in shape. He appeared to be a wealthy businessman, but his body was not going to seed from sitting in an office chair all day.

"Mom?" Christina prompted.

Margie pulled her gaze away from the larger family group to look into Christina's inquiring eyes. "Uh, sorry. Did you say something? I was distracted."

"When is Detective Riley supposed to be here? He is coming, right?"

Margie's cheeks warmed. She tried to suppress her body's reaction. She wasn't a silly schoolgirl with a crush. She was a grown woman, a professional, a homicide detective, and yes, she liked Lewis, but she didn't know for sure where their relationship was going. She had invited him to the family picnic on a whim, but she was regretting it.

It wasn't like Christina was upset about it. She hadn't complained about an intruder on their family fun. She seemed to like Lewis and didn't show any jealousy at Margie's attention being taken by someone else. But Margie felt vulnerable and was anxious that things would go well.

"He should be here any time," she told Christina casually, checking the time on the face of her phone. She glanced toward the road that wound around to all the parking areas, looking for his car. "As long as nothing came up. Sometimes our plans get derailed by a call."

Christina snorted. "Like I don't know that!"

Margie looked toward her grandfather. "Are you warm enough, Moushoom? Do you want a blanket?"

He looked thin in the wheelchair. He had always been a small man, probably the result of poor nutrition in his child-

2

hood. As he aged, he was shrinking still more. She didn't like to see him diminishing in front of her eyes. If only people didn't have to decline as they got older. She wanted him to be there forever, her strong, spry, energetic grandfather. But that man was fading.

"I am fine," Moushoom insisted, giving her a broad smile. "I'm here with my daughters, enjoying the outdoors instead of being cooped up inside, and I don't need another blanket." He smoothed the one she had already laid across his thin legs to keep him toasty. He wasn't moving around like she was, generating heat with her activity.

Moushoom took a deep breath and let it out, smiling. His eyes went over to the family that Margie had been watching earlier. "What a beautiful family. They must be so happy to all be together."

"We are still going to get the cousins together, aren't we, Mom?" Christina asked, even though she knew very well that they hoped to get the extended family together during the summer. Since Margie and Christina had moved to Calgary in the midst of the COVID lockdown, they had been unable to get together for a large gathering. Restrictions had eased by now, and many people had returned to their previous practices, but Margie was still nervous about the risks of a large gathering. COVID was not gone, despite the creation of the vaccines, and it could easily kill an old man like Moushoom. She was terrified any time there was a viral outbreak at his care center.

"Yes, of course," she agreed. "We will get together as many of the Alberta cousins as we can and have a big party."

"Good," Christina pronounced. "It will be a lot bigger than that party." She indicated their picnicking neighbors with her gaze and looked smug. The extended Patenaude family was considerably larger than the one next to them.

They would have to reserve a venue, rather than just hoping to find a free table as they had today.

"It's not how big a family is that matters," Margie pointed out. "It is how close they are. What their relationships are like. They all seem to be getting along pretty well."

But appearances could be deceiving, and it turned out there was a lot more going on at the neighboring family's picnic than Margie imagined.

The smiling faces and warm, cheerful voices were as misleading as the mirrored surface of the reservoir. It looked as smooth as glass, hiding the danger beneath the surface.

CHAPTER TWO

*S*tella started barking wildly, making Margie jump. She automatically patted her leg to call the dog to her and looked around to see what had agitated her. The midsize dog, mostly brown, was focused on something across the green space.

"Come here, Stella. What is it?"

Stella did not look back at her, continuing to bark. But her ears were forward, curious and welcoming, rather than alarmed or aggressive.

Margie thought at first that Stella had seen a squirrel, but then saw the long-legged man walking across the green grass toward them, a friendly smile on his face.

"Oh, here he is," she told Christina, who, of course, could see with her own eyes. Christina rolled her big brown eyes and busied herself with unpacking more food from the cooler.

"It looks like this is the right place," Lewis told Margie with a big smile. "The park is certainly hopping today."

"Yeah, good thing it isn't dead," Christina quipped. "Or Mom would have to get to work."

"Well, Detective Parks Pat is on the scene," Lewis acknowledged, "she wouldn't have to go too far."

"No dead bodies today," Margie declared. "No accidents, no homicides, just people enjoying the warm spring day, each other's company, and the beauty of nature."

Lewis nodded and gave Margie a friendly smile. He didn't shake her hand or hug her, both of them a little awkward and not sure how to handle the relationship. They were not a couple and this was not a date. They were just friends. Detective Lewis Riley had been invited along as an afterthought when Margie had realized that, back from his latest undercover job, he would be spending Victoria Day by himself. Margie didn't think he should be alone. He needed to be surrounded by friends, to be able to relax in a gathering where he didn't have to pretend to be anything other than what he was.

"Can I help you with anything?" Lewis offered, dispelling the awkward moment.

"I think we've got everything under control," Margie said, looking around. "Just waiting for the fire to burn down a bit so we have some good coals and can get the perfect roasted hot dogs."

Lewis looked at the fire, and to his credit, he did not see the need to grab one of the wiener sticks and push the logs around to "fix" her fire. "Looks great. It's about time I had a good cookout. Thank you for inviting me."

"Christina, Moushoom, you remember Detective Riley?" Margie introduced, though, of course, they all knew who the others were. But they had only met a time or two, and Margie thought it was important to repeat names, for her grandfather especially, to make sure they knew each other.

"Welcome to our fire," Moushoom said, and held out one gnarled hand for Lewis.

Lewis took it and shook gently. "Thank you, Sir."

"Sir," Moushoom chuckled. "We've come a long way from what cops used to call an Indian."

Lewis nodded and smiled. "I hope so," he agreed, "Sir."

Moushoom smiled at that and fingered his Métis sash. He had not worn it as a young man, but it was a badge of honor now, and he showed off his heritage proudly every opportunity he got with the colorful woven sash and other traditional clothing.

CHAPTER THREE

*H*ot dogs followed, accompanied by an assortment of salads and fruits, bannock prepared in a frying pan over the fire, soft drinks and lemonade, chips, and, of course, toasted marshmallows for dessert. Margie could not have asked for it to unfold better. She was relaxed and happy to be with her family and Detective Lewis Riley, who turned out to be an expert wiener roaster and harmonica player. Margie shook her head in amazement. She never would have predicted the harmonica.

The family at the next fire became increasingly noisy as the day drew on. Unlike Margie's family picnic, theirs included a decent amount of alcohol. Since Calgary Parks had recently begun allowing alcohol in designated areas, Margie couldn't say anything about it unless they got really rowdy.

There had been raised voices for a while, people getting a bit aggressive with each other, but Lewis and Margie had kept an eye on things, and it hadn't turned physical. Eventually, the group started to break up, with members going in different directions. Only a few remained, unwinding, cleaning up, packing up the leftover food and equipment.

Moushoom was asleep and Margie had no desire to interrupt his nap. They could stay as long as they needed to. When he woke up, they would head back to the nursing home, see that he was settled, and then go home.

It was starting to cool off, so Margie slipped on a jacket, put a blanket around her snoozing grandfather's shoulders, and pulled her chair a little closer to the dying fire.

"What's going on over there?" Lewis murmured.

Margie followed his gaze to the other picnic site. She didn't ask what Lewis was talking about, but watched the people still there, analyzing their behavior.

A middle-aged woman looked at her watch and spoke sharply to her husband. Margie couldn't make out her words. Her husband looked around and shrugged.

"He should be back by now," the woman said, her voice rising loudly enough that Margie could make it out clearly this time.

"He's a grown man. He can take care of himself. Better than most of us, I might add."

"Something still could have happened to him. He should have been back by now. He never takes this long." Another look at her watch. "Especially when he knows someone is waiting for him."

The man smirked. "Maybe he's trying to teach you a lesson. Cross him, get in his way, and he makes you wait and worry."

"Well, what am I supposed to do about it? Just sit here and pretend that I'm not worried? He could have had a heart attack."

Margie exchanged looks with Lewis. Christina was tapping away on her phone, but Margie saw her pause for a moment as she, too, became aware of the concerns being raised at the next picnic area.

"Maybe we should call someone," the woman said. "How do you call a park ranger? Do they even have them here?"

"Maybe 9-1-1," her husband said. "But I really don't think it is an emergency, do you? He just went farther than he expected and is taking longer to get back."

Margie looked at Lewis, sighed, and stood up. She approached the couple, crossing the invisible barrier between the two picnic sites.

"I'm sorry, I don't mean to eavesdrop, but I couldn't help overhearing…" Margie held out her hand to introduce herself. "I'm Detective Patenaude with the Calgary Police."

"Oh!" The woman's eyes widened in shock. "I never would have thought *you* were a cop."

Margie was aware of the lack of Indigenous representation on the police force. Of course it was a surprise for someone to see her dark skin and native features and find out she was a police detective.

The woman, in her fifties or early sixties, hesitated only an instant before shaking Margie's proffered hand. "I'm Fiona. And this is my husband, Victor Li."

The husband was Asian. Margie wasn't sure of his racial origins further than that. She was not adept at sorting Chinese features from Japanese or other Asian ancestry. And in Canada, it was often a racial mix anyway. He nodded but didn't offer his hand, so Margie didn't offer hers.

"Can we be of any help?"

Margie spoke for Lewis, who had followed her, not introducing him, but letting Fiona draw her own conclusions. Lewis might want to remain in the background, unnamed, even though he had come over to see if his help was needed.

Fiona frowned at her watch again, trying to decide whether she was really concerned or not. Finally, she nodded.

"Well… I don't know who to call otherwise; at least you could point us in the right direction. My father, Richard O'Connor, went kayaking… and hasn't returned. It's been longer than he usually goes. He said he'd be back by now." She immediately started to argue against her own concern. "Of course, he might have just stopped to talk to someone. Maybe he ran into one of his kayaking buddies."

"He's in really good shape," Victor offered. "I'm sure he's just fine. He goes paddling all the time. Almost every day, once the season opens. I wouldn't expect anything to happen to an expert out there."

Margie looked out at the reservoir. She couldn't see any kayaks on the water. She could see a rowboat on the other side, but there were not many people in the water today. Despite how much Margie had enjoyed the warm spring weather, the temperature was now dropping and the wind picking up. The water must still be close to zero degrees, even if there wasn't a layer of ice on top.

"We should get someone out looking for him," she told Lewis. "If he's just talking to a friend, no harm done. But if he is sick or hurt, we need to get to him as quickly as possible."

Lewis nodded. "I assume you have tried to call him?" he asked Fiona.

"Yes, I tried, but he doesn't answer his phone when he's out there. He puts it on Do Not Disturb and doesn't look at it until he gets out of the water. He would just leave it in the car or a locker, but he says he needs to have it with him in case of emergency. So if something goes wrong, he can call for help." She folded her arms, still looking anxious. "I suppose it's good that he hasn't called, but…" She shook her head. "I get more worried the longer it is. What if something happened and he *couldn't* call?"

"Does he share his location with you?" Margie suggested.

Fiona rolled her eyes dramatically. "No, of course not. That's an invasion of privacy. Then how are we supposed to know if something happens to him? How are we supposed to find him?"

"I'll call for water rescue," Lewis said. "If he's in the water, we need the experts out there ASAP. You get CPS and park authorities on board." He paused, giving her a little smile. "I assume you know who to call, Parks Pat."

Margie shook her head at him, but she laid a comforting hand on Fiona's arm to assure her they knew what they were doing. "We will get the ball rolling," she promised. "What about the rest of your family? Are you the only one still here?"

"Me and Victor, yes," Fiona said. She looked around as if they might rematerialize.

"Why don't you start calling them? Just see whether anyone saw what direction he went or knew what his plans were more exactly. They can come back to help with the search if they are able. You probably know where he is most likely to be in the park. If he kayaked every day, he must have had favorite spots. Did he always launch from the same place? Take the same route? Come out in the same place? You can put your heads together and compile what you know, okay? We'll have Calgary Search and Rescue out here in minutes. The more guidance you can give them, the better."

Fiona nodded. She bit her lip and brought her phone up in front of her. "I'll start calling everyone back," she confirmed.

Margie walked back to her own picnic site to check on Moushoom and Christina. Christina watched her approach, eyebrows up. "What's going on?"

"The man who was eating over there? The grandfather? It looks like he is missing. Temporarily, anyway. We are rallying the troops."

Christina looked over at Moushoom, still asleep in his wheelchair.

"That would be awful! What happened?"

"He went kayaking." At Christina's disbelieving look, Margie shrugged. "He looked very fit. His daughter says that he kayaks every day."

"The white-haired guy that was over there?"

"Yes."

"Wow. Yeah, he looked like he was in really good shape; I was thinking how nice it would be if…" Christina looked at Moushoom. "If *he* was in such good shape. He can't be that much older."

"The great-grandkids over there were quite young, so Moushoom is probably at least ten years older."

Christina nodded. "Still, I wish he was in that kind of shape."

"Of course. So do I. But we have to each accept the stage of life each of us is at. I have to work the phones for a while, so will you keep an eye on Moushoom? Explain what is going on if he wakes up and check to make sure he's not getting cold? Give me a heads-up if he needs to be taken back to the nursing home. I'll pass the baton to someone else. This isn't my wheelhouse anyway."

"Parks Pat," Christina teased.

"Parks Pat doesn't do search and rescue," Margie said wryly. "At least, I'm not an expert at it. I'll pass it on to the people who are. We will leave once everything is under control."

"Okay. I'll watch Moushoom," Christina agreed.

"Thank you."

Margie sat down and dialed 9-1-1 to get the appropriate agencies to coordinate a search.

CHAPTER FOUR

*L*uckily, the days were getting long, so they had plenty of daylight for a search, even though it was early evening by the time the parties started to assemble.

The boathouse manager confirmed the time that Richard O'Connor had been at the boathouse to take his kayak out and that he hadn't returned.

"I was getting a little concerned," Emily said, looking at the timepiece that hung around her neck. "Mr. O'Connor isn't usually out for that long, and he didn't say he was going to do anything different than usual."

"How long is he usually out?" Margie asked.

"An hour. Maybe two, if it is a really nice day and he just couldn't pull himself away. But this long..." She looked at the digital face of the timer again. "No, never this long. I knew today was his big picnic with his family, so I thought maybe he figured he needed to work off extra calories or he needed longer to unwind. But I was just thinking about talking to Member Services about what I should do."

Emily seemed concerned that they would think she

hadn't done her job. But Margie didn't know what more could have been expected of her. She wasn't there to babysit the adults who chose to go out kayaking, whether for a short paddle or a long one.

"Don't you worry," the Calgary Search and Rescue coordinator assured her. "We're going to find him." He entered the time Richard O'Connor had left the boathouse in the chart on his clipboard. "And as far as you know, no one saw or heard from him after this? You didn't take a break in the afternoon and might have missed him coming back?"

"His kayak is still gone," Emily pointed to an empty rack on the wall. "If he had come back when I went to the bathroom or was helping someone else, it would be right there."

"What route did he normally take?"

"I don't know…" She shook her head. "Maybe clockwise… but I didn't watch him once he was in the water. That's just an impression."

The CANSARA coordinator nodded and noted it on his chart, sketching out a general route and deciding where to deploy the searchers.

But as it turned out, the search never deployed in full force. One of the rowing coaches who knew the reservoir well had headed out on the water as soon as he heard that Richard O'Connor had not returned, and it was right about that time that his call for assistance came over the emergency frequency.

"Bart Hanson requesting assistance. Found the missing kayak. Victim non-responsive. Need EMS."

He relayed his GPS coordinates.

A buzz of excitement and concern went out over those who had gathered for the search. The radio stayed silent until the fire department water rescue responded.

"Water rescue is on the way. ETA five minutes. Is the victim breathing?"

"Negative," Hanson responded. "No breath sounds detected. But the body is ice cold."

Margie knew Richard O'Connor would not be declared dead until they'd had a chance to warm the body up, unless there was a catastrophic injury. Heart and respiration could be slowed so much as to be undetectable when the body was cold.

She listened to the exchanges over the emergency frequency for a few minutes until water rescue arrived and confirmed that they were bringing the body ashore. Hanson would tow the empty kayak back to the boathouse.

Margie gazed out at the glassy surface of the water. The beauty of the day was lost on her now. As peaceful as the water looked from a distance, Margie could never get close to a large body of water like this without her throat starting to close and her heart pounding wildly. She would never be a kayaker. She wasn't even sure if she could get onto a ferry or cruise ship, where she could be on the water without having to actually see it. She would still *know*.

Water was deadly. It would swallow up whatever and whoever it could.

As calm and innocuous as it looked, the water could not be trusted.

CHAPTER FIVE

*A*fter ensuring EMS would deal directly with Fiona and the rest of the family members who had returned to the scene, Margie headed back to her family.

Moushoom was awake now, playing a game of cards with Christina. Neither seemed to have suffered from having to hang out in the park for the extra time while Margie and Lewis had been dealing with the search for the missing kayaker.

"Hi, sweetie; thanks for being so patient." Margie dropped a kiss on Christina's forehead. "Do you want to finish your hand before we go?"

"Yes," Christina said. "I think I've got him this time."

Moushoom looked sly. "Don't count your chickens before they're hatched."

"Old Indian proverb?" Margie teased.

He chuckled. Margie sat down to wait for them to finish.

"I'd better be going too," Lewis told her, lingering a few extra minutes. "This wasn't quite what I was expecting when you asked me if I wanted to come to a picnic."

"Yeah… it wasn't quite what I had planned, either. But at

least they waited until after we were finished eating. I still had a good time."

"Maybe next time we could go out on the reservoir ourselves," Lewis suggested. "If you're not turned off by what happened today."

Christina looked at him. "What happened?" she asked. "Did you find him?"

Lewis looked at Margie for her answer, unsure how she wanted him to answer Christina.

"They found him," Margie said slowly. "But unfortunately... he'd had a medical emergency. We won't know the final outcome right away, but it doesn't look good."

"You think he's going to die?"

Margie nodded and didn't explain the ins and outs of cold-water drowning. "Unfortunately, I think we were too late. But you never know. Miracles do happen."

Christina looked at Moushoom, maybe remembering how just a few hours ago, she had been wishing that he was still active and vigorous like Richard O'Connor. Now O'Connor was gone. It was a sobering thought.

"I feel bad for his family."

"Yes, me too," Margie agreed.

They played their game, with Moushoom again beating his great-granddaughter and laughing about it.

"I don't know how you do it!" Christina complained. "Is he cheating, Mom?"

Margie held up her hands. "Don't ask me his secrets. He'll take those to the grave with him. Let's get the car packed."

Lewis helped them carry the coolers and other supplies to the car, with Margie working out how to stack everything to make it fit like a jigsaw puzzle. Or maybe a game of Tetris or Jenga.

Lewis leaned over Margie as she slid into the driver's seat.

"You didn't answer my question about going for a paddle on the reservoir," he pointed out.

Margie sighed. She did want to spend more time with him and get to know him better, but boating would be a much bigger problem than he knew. "I'm afraid… I'm not a big fan of the water," she admitted. Her face burned, and she couldn't meet his eyes.

"You're not a fan of the water?" he repeated. "What does that mean?"

Christina finished settling Moushoom into his seat and wedged his wheelchair into the space they'd left for it. She motioned Stella to jump in and squashed herself into the little space left for her.

"It means she's afraid of the water."

Lewis looked surprised. He looked at Margie's face. "Really? Is that true?"

Margie nodded miserably. "Yes. I know it's silly and ridiculous. You're perfectly safe on the water if you follow all the proper precautions. But tell my amygdala that."

He chuckled. "Okay. I withdraw the invitation. We'll do something else next time."

Margie smiled in appreciation. "Thank you. I'd love to do something else."

He shut her door and patted the top of the car to indicate she was good to go. Margie pulled out, waved goodbye to him, and started on the route home. She rolled her eyes and shook her head. *I'd love to do something else?* Had she really said that?

"He's nice, Mom," Christina offered.

"Yes, he is," Margie agreed.

"Are you guys dating now?"

"Not exactly. We'll see where it goes."

"It would be nice for you to have a man in your life,"

Moushoom contributed, smiling. "It's always nice to have someone looking after you."

Margie wasn't sure she was looking for someone to take care of her. That could complicate things. But it was nice to have a friend.

"Don't everybody marry me off yet," Margie said. "I'm not even sure where it is going to go. We don't know yet whether we are compatible or not. Just let us take things slowly and see how it works out. I'm not sure I want to date another cop. Especially an undercover cop. He spends a lot of time out of contact."

"You do what makes you happy," Moushoom told Margie, patting her hand.

CHAPTER SIX

*A*fter a couple of hours at home, Margie was starting to relax. Her cop brain was beginning to calm down and realize she was at home and didn't have to be hypervigilant anymore. Her phone rang, and she picked it up to look at the caller ID.

Police dispatcher.

Margie tried to calm the immediate racing of her heart and tell herself that they were just following up on something to do with Richard O'Connor's accident. She swiped to accept the call.

"Detective Patenaude."

"Detective Pat. I hear you're finding your own bodies on vacation again."

Margie cleared her throat. "Not exactly, but I was involved in the search and rescue this afternoon."

"The hospital has confirmed that Richard O'Connor passed away. Which means that we are opening an investigation into his death."

Margie could see what was coming. "And you want to

know if I want to be primary on it, since I was involved from the beginning of the search."

"You are the one who placed the initial call, and you are a homicide detective."

"Umm… okay," Margie agreed. "Are you sending anyone over to take evidence at the boathouse? Do I need to be somewhere tonight?"

"You're okay tonight. No one can access it until they open tomorrow. You can coordinate with one of the death investigators from the Office of the Chief Medical Examiner to be there when it opens."

She sighed. At least she didn't have to go out again tonight.

"All right," she told the dispatcher, "He can call or text me, and we'll set something up."

"You should know that the boathouse manager made a statement of Mr. O'Connor not being himself when he took out his boat today."

Margie's attention, which had been drifting, snapped back to the conversation.

"What? She didn't say anything like that while I was there."

"I believe she will be available for you to interview her tomorrow. But I thought you'd better be aware from the start that the circumstances are already… complex."

"Well… I appreciate that." Margie only wished that he had said something before she had accepted the assignment thinking it would be a clear-cut accidental death. And maybe it still would. But she would have to approach every step very carefully.

MARGIE WAS UP EARLY to make sure she would be able to be at the boathouse when the club opened to ensure that any evidence was carefully preserved.

She eyed Lester, the tall, lanky death investigator, who didn't look any older than Christina. Professionals like doctors seemed to be getting younger and younger all the time.

"Hi. Detective Patenaude," she introduced herself. "Some people prefer Detective Pat."

"Or Parks Pat," he suggested.

"Oh, I guess someone has filled you in on my alter ego. Yes, sometimes known as Parks Pat." She made a gesture to indicate her environment. "When I happen to be actually in a park."

He grinned. "And is it true you were here yesterday when the deceased was discovered?"

"Worse... I picnicked next to Mr. O'Connor and his family, initiated the search when he didn't come back from kayaking, and yes, was here when they found his body."

"Someone might actually think you were involved in his death."

"Don't say that, even joking. I don't need to be a suspect in a suspicious death."

He shrugged and nodded.

Emily, the blond young woman she had talked to the day before arrived to unlock the boathouse. She kept her head down, not meeting Margie's eyes.

"You and I need to talk after we've finished processing the boat," Margie told her.

The blonde turned quite pink. "I know," she agreed.

"Good. Make some time for me. Be sure someone is available to cover for you while we talk."

"Okay."

Emily swung the door open for Margie and Lester and

reached around the doorframe to flick on the lights. Margie's eyes were immediately drawn to O'Connor's kayak, back in place in the rack.

"That's the one, right?"

Emily nodded. "Yeah. That's the kayak he was in yesterday."

Margie cocked her head slightly. "Did he have another one?"

"The one above it is his too. He would pick which one he wanted to use. Or sometimes he would come in with someone else, and they would go together."

"He had a buddy he paddled with?"

"Not always the same person. Sometimes someone from his family. Sometimes a friend or someone he worked with. I didn't always know who they were."

"And yesterday? Was he by himself?"

"Oh, yes," she agreed. "Just Mr. O'Connor."

"Okay, thanks."

There wasn't much for Margie to do as Lester went over the boat an inch at a time, looking for any trace evidence. Any blood, dings to the boat, or any substance that needed to be accounted for. But he didn't find anything of note. Richard O'Connor had not, it appeared, been bashed over the head while in the boat or suffered any other violence that had left any trace behind.

"It all looks pretty straightforward," Lester said with a shrug, finally standing up and returning the kayak to its rack. "He probably had a heart attack or stroke."

"Probably something simple like that," Margie agreed. "I'll need to talk to the boathouse manager about her statement. Do you want to stay for that?"

He apparently did not. He said he would take the few swabs and fibers he had retrieved from the boat to the lab, and it would be a few days before they were processed and the results were back. Just as was always the case. Margie was familiar with timelines. A few days was good. She didn't like having to wait weeks or months for results. That made her anxious.

When Margie had finished in the boathouse and Lester was on his way back to OCME to get his evidence logged and processed, Emily was ready to talk. She had gotten permission to use one of the rooms at the Rowing Club so they could have the interview in private, which Margie thought showed initiative.

She studied the younger woman as they sat down to talk. Emily was blond and athletic, with a slim build. She looked barely old enough to have graduated high school, but Margie knew by her credentials that she had already finished college. She had gotten her degree in business administration, and the job at the Rowing Club had grown out of a summer job helping with rowing lessons—not as the teacher, but as a second pair of eyes and hands making sure that everybody in the class was safe as the teacher gave his instructions and led the students through the various exercises.

After getting an outline of Emily's credentials and history at the club, Margie guided her gently into what had happened the previous day when Richard O'Connor arrived at the boathouse to get his kayak.

"I noticed that he was different than usual," Emily admitted. "But I didn't think much about it. I mean… just because he was having an 'off' day, I didn't think that meant… that he was going to die. I just thought… he'd had a good time with his family that day."

"What do you mean?" Margie pressed, frowning, "A good time with his family?"

"Well, I mean… just that he seemed like… maybe he'd had a bit to drink while he was with them."

Margie could remember the drinks flowing freely at the

picnic site next to hers. And she could remember how the babel of voices rose as the day went on, morphing into irritation and arguments by the end of what should have been a pleasant family get-together. There hadn't been any violence. No pushing, no one taking a swing, but there had definitely been disagreement over something. Everyone had not been happy at the party.

"Did you smell alcohol on him?" she asked Emily.

"Umm…" she could see Emily reviewing the memory, playing it back, thinking over each impression. "No, I couldn't smell any alcohol. He had on… like… deodorant or aftershave. Or cologne. Something nice. Not too overpowering. But I couldn't smell any alcohol. It would have been covered up by the scent unless it was really strong."

"Okay. Good observation. So what made you think he'd had too much to drink?"

"Just… he seemed a little wobbly. A little loose. Like he had to steady himself on the doorframe as he walked through it. Nothing big, not staggering. Just… he wasn't usually like that. He was usually very…" Emily struggled to find the right word to convey what she had seen. "Confident, I guess? Like he didn't have any hesitation when he moved. But yesterday… he might have been tired, or had an ear infection that gave him a little vertigo. Something like that."

"But your first instinct was that he had been drinking."

"Yes." Emily nodded. She chewed on her lip, trying to decide whether she should say something else, but did not add anything to her answer in the end.

"Did you notice anything else about him that might have suggested he'd had something to drink? Or was that it?"

"His eyes, I guess. I don't hang out with people who drink or do drugs. When he came in from outside, he went from the sunshine into the boathouse, where the lights aren't that great. Everyone's eyes take a minute to adjust. But I really noticed his. Like, they were big. Really big."

"His pupils were dilated."

Emily looked unsure of this, but nodded.

"So with that, and him being a little unsteady, you thought maybe he'd had a lot to drink with his family."

"Yes. But I didn't think much of it. I didn't think that he was too impaired to paddle. He was an experienced kayaker. He was out there all the time. I just *noticed*, that's all. I wasn't concerned."

Margie nodded. Emily had already said more than the management would have liked. If the Parks Department or the Rowing Club had heard what she had to say, they would have been protesting loudly and trying to keep it under wraps. They didn't want the family coming back to them and saying they were liable for O'Connor's death because Emily had let him boat after observing signs of impairment.

"I appreciate you sharing that with me," Margie told her. "We'll need you to sign a written statement, just to get this all on the record, okay?"

Emily nodded.

"Good. Did Mr. O'Connor talk about anything? You knew he'd come from a family picnic, so he must have told you something about it."

"I guess so... he'd been talking about it before, too. Last week. Saying that he was excited to be getting the whole clan together. I gathered that... they didn't always get along. Maybe some of them hadn't seen each other for a while."

Margie made a note of this. "And is that all he said? Was there anything else?"

"I asked if he'd had a good time... He said it was a family thing, like that meant it wasn't exactly fun." She shrugged. "I know how that is. Family reunions... it seems like they always end with arguments and resentments."

"Did he tell you how long he was going out for or what route he was going to take?"

"No. He never did, so that wasn't unusual. I mean, sometimes he would say what a lovely day it was, and I would guess he would be longer that day. But he didn't say how long he would be or when he would be getting back."

"And did he say it was a lovely day yesterday?"

"He said it was warm… I think that's all."

"And did you take that to mean he would take a longer paddle?"

"No."

She had good intuition. Margie would say that for her.

"Was there anything else you can think of? Anything unusual? Anything that made you think that he was impaired or unhappy? Anything?"

"No, I don't think so."

Margie nodded. She gave Emily her business card. "Let me know if you think of anything else. In the meantime, we should get your statement typed up…"

"I can do that," Emily offered. "I've got a computer here. Then it will be all out of the way." She sighed. "I really don't want to have to think about it anymore. Though I know everyone will be asking me about it for the next week or two."

"Well, you can try telling them you don't want to talk about it… I don't know if that will help. Sometimes, when you hold back, people are just that much more insistent about finding out the details."

"Yeah, I know." She sighed.

"Well, if you want to go type that up right now, I'll stick around and witness it for you. Then I shouldn't need to bother you again unless there is something in it that needs further clarification."

"Okay. You want to just wait in here?"

"Unless someone else needs the room."

"No. That's okay. You can stay here. I'll be back in a few minutes."

After Emily excused herself, Margie gave the Office of the Chief Medical Examiner a call.

"It's Detective Patenaude. I know the answer is probably no, but has anyone had a chance to do the autopsy on Mr. O'Connor?"

"Oh, Dr. Galt was working on that one. I think he's finished. Let me see if I can transfer you to him."

There was dead air for a few minutes, followed by a few clicks.

"Detective Parks Pat?" Dr. Galt inquired.

"That's me," Margie agreed, shaking her head. "I'm calling about Richard O'Connor."

"Your boating accident."

"Yes."

"Well, first things first, and that is that it is usual for water to be found in the lungs of a drowning victim."

"Of course," Margie agreed.

"But Mr. O'Connor did not have water in his lungs."

Margie felt her own lungs deflate and a sick feeling of anticipation settled into her stomach.

"So he didn't die from drowning."

"No," Dr. Galt agreed. "He did not drown in the reservoir. There was, however, some fluid in his lungs."

"Does that mean he was drowned somewhere else?"

"I don't believe it was enough to cause his death, so no. But it does look like he aspirated a small amount of vomit. So there was something else going on here."

"I just interviewed a witness who thought he might have been impaired. With alcohol. Except that he didn't smell like alcohol."

"No. His body didn't either. I have ordered a tox screen,

which will show you whether he had alcohol in his system and how much."

"Great. That will be helpful. It would be good to know just what we're looking at here."

"I will get back to you as soon as I know for sure. But for the moment... keep an open mind as to the cause of death."

CHAPTER SEVEN

Fiona O'Connor-Li was not happy about having to come in and answer questions about her father and what had happened the previous day.

The woman had to be fifty, but acted as if she were still twenty, just starting out, learning how to get along with people, carefree when she really wasn't. Margie got the feeling that she had been acting this role for a number of years. Just what was going on in Fiona's life that required a constant charade?

"Thank you for coming in," Margie told her. "And I am very sorry for your loss. I know it has been quite a shock to lose your father this way."

"It has," Fiona agreed. "I'm still not sure what's going on. He died in a kayaking accident, so I'm not sure why I needed to come here to answer any questions. Questions about what? How much of an expert he was? He'd been kayaking for years."

"You may not know this, but whenever someone dies who isn't under the care of a doctor, the death has to be investigated. It doesn't necessarily mean there is anything

31

suspicious about the case. Just that it needs a pair of eyes on it to make sure that everything is what it appears to be. In this case… no one was there to witness the incident, so we have to build a picture of what happened based on what we can learn from other people in his life."

"I don't know how I can help you with that, since I didn't see him regularly. In fact, I never went kayaking with him. I wasn't interested in it."

Margie put Fiona's name and the date at the top of the page in her notepad.

"We'll just get a few general facts down, okay? I'm sure this won't take very long."

Fiona rolled her eyes.

"Now, you're the first one I'm talking to, because you are who I talked to at the park. You're my point person. So, could you give me a general overview of the family? Are you the oldest sibling?"

"No!" Fiona laughed. "I'm the youngest. The oldest is Michael. Then Vi. Then David, and me last."

"How did you end up in charge of the family picnic? Is it just your thing? Usually, that falls to the oldest or the oldest girl."

"I was in charge of the *cleanup*. Because I'm the youngest. I can't handle anything more important than getting rid of the garbage. Even if I am a caterer by profession!"

The bitterness in Fiona's voice was obvious. If Margie hadn't already known that there were some problems between the family members because of the stuff she had heard from her picnic site, it would have been revealed now. Fiona clearly had some sibling issues, if not parental ones. And from the fact that she said she rarely saw her family, Margie had to assume that the same was true of Fiona's relationship with her parents. There were some long-festering wounds there.

"And I didn't ask about your mother. Was she there…?"

"No, Mother died a number of years ago. She was never really as healthy as Dad. She just kind of… faded away. I don't think… he really cared. Maybe that's just me having an immature view of their relationship, not understanding how close they were. But I never felt like they had much of a relationship at all. Mom had us, so they obviously had a physical relationship, but I didn't think he ever supported her emotionally, and they never did anything together."

"I'm sorry to hear that. It can be traumatizing to be orphaned, even as an adult. To suddenly no longer have either parent in your life."

"I felt like that when Mother died. Not now."

Margie nodded to acknowledge this.

"And was everyone at the picnic yesterday? All of your siblings?"

"Yes, they were all there. And some of the grandkids." Fiona thought about it. "And… Aunt Brenda and Uncle Paddy. And Dr. Helen Chang."

"Who is Dr. Chang?"

"She is a psychiatrist. A family friend, who has counseled a few of the members of the family separately. So you see, there was a doctor present," Fiona smiled. "So you don't need to have his death investigated after all."

Margie chuckled. "I wish that was the way it worked," she said. "But we're going to have to do this the right way."

Fiona sighed. She slumped in her seat. "So ask away," she ordered. "Let's get this done."

Margie got everyone's contact details from Fiona. Or whatever she had, anyway; she confessed that some of the phone numbers were older and might not work anymore.

"You have said or implied that you didn't have a very good relationship with your father. Why was that?"

"Because he was self-absorbed. He was this big oil exec and didn't care about anyone but himself. Don't be fooled by the family picnic. That wasn't done for the kids or family unity. That was just... him showing off. Showing off how here he is, this great success. Successful father, businessman, kayaker. It was a wonder he didn't have the media there. I guess he wasn't able to convince them that there was anything to see. Too bad for him. All he could do was to posture for us, and none of us cared."

"But you all went," Margie pointed out.

"Yeah... I guess we did. If we didn't, Dad would have just arranged it for a different day. Until we got it right. Best to just go when he summons you."

Margie nodded and jotted a couple of notes down.

"So you didn't have any specific beef with your father? Just that the two of you had never gotten along very well?"

Fiona nodded, but her expression was masked. "What else would there be?"

Margie studied her. "I have seen all kinds of dysfunction and abuse. You are not going to shock me."

"I don't have anything to tell you, shocking or not. We just didn't have a relationship. He never made time for relationships, so that's what he ended up with. A family full of strangers."

"I see. Well..." Margie stood slowly and handed Fiona one of her business cards. "Please call me if you remember anything or something comes up that might be relevant to the investigation. No matter how unimportant you think it might be. Sometimes very insignificant details can turn a case around."

Fiona didn't throw the card back at her and state that she

would never do anything to help Margie's investigation, no matter what, so that was a win, right?

Margie was going to count it as one.

CHAPTER EIGHT

*M*ichael O'Connor, the oldest child, was the one Margie managed to get in for an interview next. She might have to track some of the picnic attendees down and visit them in their homes or places of business.

Michael was a big man, tall and solidly built, with a large red nose. He was interested in all that he saw in the police station, but at the same time was not interested in being there and didn't appreciate having to talk to her.

Did any of Richard's family even care that he was gone?

"So, you were at the park?" he asked her. Word had apparently gotten out about how Margie had become involved in the investigation.

"Yes," Margie admitted. "My family was in the picnic site next to yours."

"I don't remember seeing you there."

He looked her over in a way that indicated he didn't think there was anything particularly memorable about her. Margie felt her face flush.

"Yes, your group seemed to take themselves quite seriously," Margie told him. "It seemed like there was a lot of… discussion going on."

His nostrils flared. He didn't like that. Margie was glad to have pricked him. What made him think he and his family were more important than Margie and hers?

Margie might not be a wealthy oil executive, but her family was close. Their relationship and happiness were just as important as his.

"Just what exactly do you need to know?" Michael asked. "I don't know why you think there is anything to investigate. An old man drowns while he is out kayaking. I don't see what the point of this interview is."

"He didn't drown."

"What?" Michael's brows drew together and he stared at her. "What do you mean he didn't drown?"

"There was no water in his lungs. He died before he went into the water."

Or, as Dr. Galt had informed her, it was possible that his throat had closed up with the shock of hitting the icy cold water, a reflex protective action, but with this throat closed, he would still not have been able to breathe, and would smother to death rather than drowning.

But Margie was assuming the more likely scenario that he had died before hitting the water.

"So…" Michael fumbled for an explanation. "Well, *obviously* he must have had a heart attack or something out there on the lake. It doesn't mean that… I or anyone in the family had anything to do with his death."

"Did I say you did?" Guilty conscience? She wondered.

"My father was in good physical shape, but you hear about things like this all the time. Athletes who collapse on the field. Just because they are in good shape, that doesn't mean they can't have a heart problem no one knows about.

Something they were born with, or damage caused by a virus or bacterial infection."

Margie nodded.

"Or he might have even had a virus yesterday," Michael pointed out. "Sometimes people don't feel any symptoms. And then... bang, they have a stroke. Or an allergic reaction. You just don't know."

"Do you think he might have had an allergic reaction to something at the picnic?"

"I don't know. The coroner would be able to tell that, wouldn't he?"

"His investigation is still ongoing. From what I've heard on other cases, it isn't always possible to tell an allergic reaction or smothering from other causes of death."

"They always can on TV," Michael pointed out.

"Yes." Margie looked at him steadily. He was an educated man. He knew that what he saw on TV wasn't true. Even the true crime shows were adapted or at least cherry-picked.

Michael reddened. "Yes, I know the difference between TV and real life," he said defensively.

"Good. So, would you like to tell me about your relationship with your father? How did the two of you get along?"

Michael looked up at the ceiling. "He was fine. He wasn't abusive or anything like that. A good provider. I assume you know all about his career. He just... wasn't really part of our lives, so none of us have had much to do with him as we've gotten older. He wasn't much of a father. But he wasn't a terrible person, either."

"There seemed to be... some *words* at the picnic. People got heated more than once. What was going on?"

"Well, some of my siblings might have more of a problem with him than I do."

"Oh?"

Michael tried to figure out what to say. "Dad didn't

38

approve of our lives, you know. We were all… pretty inde-
pendent-minded. We didn't do things just because he
thought we should. Or not do things because he thought we
shouldn't. And that caused… more than a few arguments."

"For example?"

Michael scratched the table, his eyes very focused on the
grain of the wood.

"Vi was divorced. Dad was against divorce. Word had it
that she'd had a couple of affairs in the past. I don't know all
of the details," he said virtuously. "I don't listen to gossip and
rumors."

"Of course not," Margie murmured.

"My brother, he's an *artist* and currently shacked up with
some sculptor. Alvarez, his name is. That didn't sit well with
Dad. Don't ask me why he thought he was the morality
police. It wasn't like he was the straight arrow himself. I've
heard stories. Not only that, but rumor has it he's got money
stashed in offshore accounts to avoid paying taxes."

"How did the family feel about that?"

"I got stuck with the family business. He wouldn't put
any capital into it, but he said I should be able to run it
without any outside investors now. He would have been able
to if *he'd* stayed in control."

"The family business?" Margie repeated. "Oil?"

"No. That was something *else* he went into. He was
always doing something else, putting another feather in his
cap. The family business is construction. All of us were
supposed to be involved in managing and running the
company. But they didn't want to be involved and I was not
getting paid to run everything."

"So what happened?"

"I took over all of the management. I was the only one
who was interested or capable of running it. The others were
happy to let me do it."

"So that worked out okay?"

"Except I never *wanted* to get into construction. I'm looking at selling. And Dad still has a veto on the sale. Or he did." Michael paused. "I guess he doesn't anymore."

"That's convenient."

"It's not convenient in any way," Michael growled. "None of this company stuff has been. He should have just sold it off years ago."

"How do the others feel about you selling it?"

He shrugged. "They don't know. And I'm not going to tell them. It's my company to deal with as I see fit."

"But your father still had a veto."

"He did, because it was built into the articles. But they don't. They never did. I can sell it if I want to."

"Okay." Margie scribbled down a few notes. "Is that one of the things that you guys were arguing about at the park?"

"We weren't arguing."

"There were some raised voices."

"Discussions. Not arguments."

"Okay. Was that something that was discussed yesterday?"

"The business came up," Michael admitted. "They were... irritated that I didn't have anything to share with them."

Margie looked at the notes she had for each of the family members.

"And Fiona? Were there any problems between her and your dad?"

"Fiona?" Michael shrugged. "Fiona's a good girl. I don't think Dad had any issues with her. But that husband of hers? Victor Li? I don't trust that guy. He's been helping with Dad's finances. And things don't look *regular* to me."

"You think he's up to something shady?"

"He's just that kind of guy. I don't know if he's ever

touched anything that *wasn't* shady. I didn't trust him, and if I had my way, Victor wouldn't have been involved in any of Dad's stuff."

"Why did he hire him, then?"

"A favor for Fiona, probably. She's the baby, so she gets what she wants, you know?"

"It is a pretty common pattern," Margie agreed. "But Fiona wouldn't want her husband involving her father in something shady, would she?"

"If she knew about it... no. But does she? I don't know if she realizes what kind of a guy he is."

"Have you tried to talk to her about it?"

Michael gave her a look. "You saw what it's like when we try to talk to each other, right? Yesterday was a pretty good day for us. Everyone stuck around and we had a good lunch together. Other get-togethers have not gone nearly as well."

"Were there any other topics of conversation that were... delicate? Or is that everything?"

Michael rolled his eyes and shook his head. "Any conversation could be volatile. I guess... that is probably the last time we will all be in the same place again. It was Dad who thought we should all get together. I don't think the rest of us will keep it up. It's just that none of us even like each other that much. What's the point in getting together to argue more about stuff that happened years ago?"

"Maybe you could set some ground rules about topics of conversation and dredging up old hurts."

"Who would make these rules? We would never agree to them."

Margie chuckled and nodded. "You might need a mediator," she admitted. "But people do find family reunions rewarding. Maybe it would be worth the time and effort you put into it."

"I doubt it."

"Well, okay. I didn't ask Fiona, but how did your dad look during the picnic? I mean physically? Did he have a good appetite? Did he complain about indigestion?"

Michael didn't answer at first. He considered, and shrugged.

"He looked fine to me. I mean, I should look so good at his age. Or be so active. Yesterday, I would have told you he would live to be a hundred. Or older. He would outlast all of us."

"So you didn't notice anything 'off' in his behavior or appetite?"

"He had a good appetite. I didn't notice any issues. Same Dad as always."

Margie nodded. "And was he drinking?"

"Drinking? As in alcohol? One or two, maybe. Vi brought the makings for G&T, his favorite. I don't think he had more than two. He was drinking coffee later in the afternoon."

"The boathouse manager thought that he might have been impaired. Did he often drink enough to be noticeably drunk?"

"No," Michael's tone was surprised. "He never had more than one or two. He was very careful about his body. He ate a healthy diet, exercised, never took anything. If he drank at all, it was only one or two. Maybe G&T the first time, and just tonic water after that. Or coffee, like yesterday. He would lecture us on healthy eating all the time. It might have been a picnic, but the table wasn't loaded down with cookies and Jello salad, I'll tell you that. Everyone knew better than to bring junk."

Margie frowned, writing down a few notes about his drinking and eating habits. She would have to check with his doctor and people aside from family as well, not just relying on what they said. Family members were often in denial about drinking problems.

"The boathouse manager doesn't know what he's talking about," Michael said strongly. "Dad would never drink that much."

"Do you know the boathouse manager?" Margie asked, though she already knew the answer. He didn't know that the boathouse manager was a woman, so he obviously didn't know her. But she was interested in hearing the answer.

"No, I never went kayaking with Dad. None of us did. He was devoted to it, but none of us kids got the bug. Vi's ex, Scott, he was into kayaking. He would be the one to talk to about the people at the club or any questions about how the accident might have happened. He and Dad still paddled together sometimes."

"Scott?" Margie jotted it down. "What is his last name?"

"Smith."

"But he wasn't there at the picnic yesterday?"

"No. But that doesn't mean he wasn't around the park. He was like Dad, dipped his paddle in whenever he had the chance."

Margie added this to her notes.

CHAPTER NINE

*M*argie stretched her legs and brewed another pot of coffee. Jones came into the breakroom, inhaling the entrancing odor eagerly. She settled at the counter to wait with Margie for it to finish brewing. Her wavy blond hair was escaping from her bun and bobby pins. It never would just stay neat and flat. Margie grinned at Jones's effort to tame her rebellious locks.

"Hey, you've been pretty busy in there today," Jones observed after tucking a few stray locks away. "Have you got interviews all day today?"

Margie stretched her shoulders and rubbed her temples. "It sure feels like it. And I'm not sure what the point is. I've got an apparently healthy man who died while kayaking. But he was eighty years old. Not exactly in the prime of his life. It was probably just a heart attack or stroke. If it wasn't for the boathouse manager saying that he had appeared to be intoxicated…"

"It would be open and shut? What did the postmortem show?"

"I haven't got the full results yet. Just the news that

44

O'Connor didn't have water in his lungs. I'd better check to see if Dr. Galt has finished yet." Margie checked the time. "Yeah, he's probably finished."

"I can check if you like."

"That would be great, actually. If he decides it is definitely an accident, I can probably get away with not talking to everyone present at the picnic. None of them were at the accident scene, after all."

"That you know of."

"They say none of them paddle. Only one ex-son-in-law. And he wasn't there."

"Maybe you can at least reduce the number you have to talk to."

"Yeah. Let me know what you find out. I'd better not keep my next witness waiting longer than necessary." Margie poured a couple of mugs of coffee. "You know where to find me."

Margie returned to the interview room, where Uncle Paddy and Aunt Brenda were waiting for her. She had asked them to come in only one at a time, but they had insisted that it was together or not at all.

Margie introduced herself and looked at the couple.

Both were similar in age to Richard O'Connor. His sister-in-law, Brenda O'Reilly, and her husband, Paddy. There was something familiar about Paddy, and Margie studied him, trying to figure out if she had met him somewhere else, under different circumstances. There was something very familiar about him.

"Something bothering you?" Paddy asked, his eyes twinkling.

Margie shook her head. "I have a feeling we've met, but I don't know where."

"It's always important for a cop to know where he—or she—has encountered someone before."

"Yes, I agree. So can you help me out?"

If he was someone she'd arrested before, it was crucial to remember the circumstances. And if he was a witness or someone important in another case, she might need to know those details.

"Maybe Irish mob?" Paddy suggested mischievously. "Old IRA?"

Margie shook her head. He didn't have an accent. He wasn't Irish born. "You're not IRA."

He grinned. His wife poked at him. "Paddy, you're just being a tease! This girl has no way of knowing who you are."

Margie cocked her head. It was there, just beyond her reach.

"Paddy O'Reilly," she repeated, trying to trigger her brain. Had he been in Calgary's municipal government? Or provincial politics? Was he a criminal or former law enforcement?

"Oh!" A picture gradually formed in her mind. His face, younger, in a photograph. She tried to build out around it, remembering where she had seen the picture and why it had been there. It slid into focus reluctantly, but she was triumphant when it did. "Detective Paddy O'Reilly," she said forcefully. "Retired."

He nodded, grinning away at having eluded her for a few minutes, and at being recognized.

"Your picture is on the wall," she told him.

"The wall of shame," Paddy said mournfully.

"The wall of fame," Margie corrected. "You put in years of faithful service to this city."

"Well, that's true," he admitted.

"Why didn't you tell me who you were? That whole conversation about coming in with your wife and refusing to be interviewed separately. Why didn't you just tell me who you are?"

"You're the detective. I left it up to you to figure out."

Margie shook her head. "So your wife's sister was Richard's wife." She said it slowly to make sure she got the relationship right.

"Yes. Little Evelyn Murphy. Poor girl."

It was funny to hear someone of Evelyn's age referred to as a girl. But to Paddy, that was who she had always been. His wife's kid sister.

Margie addressed Brenda, Paddy's mousy wife. "What did you think of Richard?"

"I didn't think he was anywhere near good enough for my little sister."

It hung in the air. Margie waited for more. But it was Paddy who took up the slack.

"But they had a long marriage. They had four children together. By those measures, it was a good relationship. Maybe he wasn't good enough for her. Maybe she could have done better with a man who was home more."

"He worked a lot, from what I understand."

"He did," Paddy agreed. "Didn't have much time to waste on his family. Preferred to be at the office. Or on the water. Or at some other woman's house. A man should be at home when he can be. Not choosing everything else over her."

Margie nodded and glanced at Brenda, who seemed to agree with this in principle, but shot back, "It's easy to say he should have been at home, but were you? Night shifts, undercover, task forces, interdisciplinary teams. There were *weeks* when I didn't see your face."

Paddy rubbed his chin, his cheeks pink. "Well, that wasn't by choice," he said. "That was just my career. There is only so much you can do to control it. If you want the salary and the advancement opportunities, there are things you have to do."

She nodded. "I'm sure Richard would have told you the same. He thought as long as he was providing for her, she didn't have anything to complain about. She chose to stay with him. Chose to be home with four kids while he was off fooling around with some tramp, and to put up with it. Put up and shut up."

"What happened between them isn't our business," Paddy said reasonably.

"Just because a woman stays with a man, that doesn't mean she couldn't have done better. Just that she decided to stay with her children and make the most of it." She gave him a pointed look.

"Okay," Paddy growled. "I wasn't the perfect man or perfect husband either. You probably deserved someone better, too. But I still think Richard did right by her."

Brenda shrugged. "Since they're both dead, there isn't really any point in asking, is there?" She turned back to Margie. "You want to know what I thought of him? I thought he was selfish and self-centered."

"What did the children think of him?" Margie asked. "Do you think any of them are happy to see him dead?"

"Well… being happy to see him dead isn't quite the same thing as having a hand in his death."

CHAPTER TEN

There was a soft knock at the door, and Margie turned to see Jones standing in the cracked-open doorway. She tilted her head, signaling for Jones to join them, but Jones shook her head. Margie stood up.

"Sorry, I need to see what this is about," she apologized and went to the door.

Jones did not talk to her through the crack, but opened the door the rest of the way to invite her out, and shut it firmly behind her. Ensuring there was no way that their witnesses would hear what she had to say. Once again, Margie's stomach tightened, dreading what was coming. This case just kept getting worse and worse.

"OCME rushed a tox screen and BCA," Jones said, "in light of the witness testimony that he seemed impaired."

"Great. I assume they have results back already, or you wouldn't bother to tell me."

Jones nodded. "His blood alcohol was low. He wasn't drunk. Maybe one drink an hour or two before death."

So Michael had been right about the gin and tonic.

P.D. WORKMAN

Richard had only had one or two and then had only coffee or nonalcoholic drinks in the hours before his paddle.

"So, what was it, then?" she asked Jones. "A stroke? What does Dr. Galt think?"

"He thinks it was probably the massive dose of..." Jones looked down at her notepad, "TCA. Tricyclic antidepressant."

"Antidepressant? Did he have a prescription for it?"

"Dr. Galt says not."

For a few seconds, they both just looked at each other, thinking it through. Richard overdosed on TCA, which he didn't have a prescription for. So where had he gotten it?

From all that Margie had heard so far, there was no reason to think that Richard was suicidal. He had not been depressed or despondent at the family gathering. He was someone who took care of his body and didn't believe in taking medication unless absolutely necessary.

There was, however, plenty to indicate that his relationships with everyone who had been at the picnic the day before had not been good.

If they were looking at homicide rather than Richard simply having a heart attack or stroke while he was out on the water, then Margie was going to need to step up her investigation.

She had done everything she needed to, processing the scene and evidence, even talking to the boathouse manager and the family with the possibility in mind that it could have been something other than a natural death. But knowing that it was murder put a different slant on everything she had seen or heard and how she needed to approach the investigation.

"Oh boy. Can you make some time to help me out with this case?" Margie asked Jones.

Detective Jones nodded her head immediately. "Sure," she said, "of course. This takes precedence over anything else today. What do you need me to do?"

"I'm going to need you to track down the rest of the people who were at the picnic. I didn't get good phone numbers for everyone. I figured I'd be fine just interviewing the major players. But we will need to get everyone and get them down here ASAP. If anyone won't come in, we'll go out to them. First, though, call Fiona and find out what she did with everything after she cleaned up the picnic site yesterday. She was in charge of the cleanup. Did it all go in the garbage? Does she still have any drink containers that were used? Did she save them for a refund? If it all went into the garbage, we need to know which bins were used and talk to the park about getting all the trash from those bins for evidence, assuming it has not all been collected already. If it has, we'll need to track where it went."

Jones nodded. She took out a pen and began writing down notes. "Sure. I'll get started on that. Do you want anyone back that you've already talked to?"

"Not yet... we'll have to see."

"So, who in the family has a prescription for TCA?"

"I guess I'll need to find out."

And if someone in the family was on TCA, did that make him the killer? Maybe someone else had access to it. Would someone have used their own prescription to poison Richard O'Connor? That seemed unlikely. They must have considered that it would be discovered.

"If there is a family member you can't reach, we need to consider the possibility that *they* may have overdosed," she told Jones. "So make every effort, and if someone can't be reached, have a welfare check done."

"Right. Anything else?"

"I'm sure I'll think of more, but that is everything for now."

Jones nodded and turned away from Margie to return to her desk to get started.

CHAPTER ELEVEN

*M*argie took a few slow, deep breaths, centering her thoughts and trying to get into the mental space to continue her task. She opened the door and returned to the meeting room where Uncle Paddy and Aunt Brenda waited.

Margie sat back down at the table. Paddy was watching her with quick, bright eyes.

"What has happened?" he asked. "What news did your partner have?"

Margie thought about different ways to approach the conversation. She didn't have to tell Paddy what he wanted to know. She could withhold it and just keep asking him questions as if it were a routine death investigation with nothing suspicious having shown up yet. But Paddy knew from her face and body language that something had changed. There wasn't any point trying to pull the wool over his eyes.

Margie met Brenda's eyes. "Your brother-in-law was murdered."

Her mouth fell open in shock.

"Murdered?" Paddy repeated incredulously. "How?"

"He was poisoned. And since no one else has suffered any ill effects from the picnic, he was targeted. Only intended for him."

"Yes…" Paddy's brows were knit as he considered the facts, maybe replaying the events of the previous day in his mind. "You're sure this poison was given to him during the picnic?"

Margie had not talked to Dr. Galt to find out how long the antidepressant would have taken to kill him. Was it possible that he had taken it earlier in the day? Or swallowed a bottle of pills before heading out in the kayak? She would stay open to those possibilities until she had a chance to find out, but they didn't seem likely.

She didn't answer Paddy's question. He was an experienced detective. Let him think it over.

"Who had the opportunity to put something into Richard's food or drink without him realizing it?" Margie asked. "What kept anyone else from being poisoned?"

Brenda looked at her husband worriedly. "We didn't see anything. I can't imagine that it could be anyone in the family. Couldn't it have been accidental? Or something that Richard took? Maybe it was food poisoning."

Margie shook her head. "It was intentional."

She said it with more confidence than she had based on the facts. She was focusing on the information she needed to gather. If it turned out that Richard had taken something himself, MacDonald would not censure her for gathering the information she needed to prove whether it was or was not a family member who had killed him. He would certainly have something to say if she slacked off on the questioning because she was hoping it was suicide or one of the players was a retired cop.

Paddy looked at his wife, then back at Margie.

"We should help her out," Brenda said doubtfully. "Even if it *was* someone in the family."

"It's *your* family. I don't want to do something that hurts you."

Brenda steeled herself, pressing her lips together. "The truth is what is important. If it was someone at the picnic, we need to know that. We need to know who, and we need to do whatever we can to make sure that justice is served. We didn't come here to protect anyone."

Paddy nodded slowly. He took a deep breath and released it slowly. "Okay, from the top… Vi brought gin and tonic. That's Richard's drink. No one else was interested in it, and it isn't exactly traditional picnic fare. The bitterness of the tonic water would cover the taste of most poisons."

Margie nodded. She had already been thinking the same thing. It was the obvious answer. But they needed to look at more than just the obvious answers.

"Was that Vi's idea, or did someone ask her to bring it? Did anyone else pour the drinks or get close to the tonic water?"

"Probably." He closed his eyes, envisioning it. "Brenda and I stuck with juice. We didn't go anywhere near the drinks. Fiona brought us the juice."

"So that put Fiona at the drinks table at least once."

"Multiple times," Paddy agreed. "She was performing bar service most of the afternoon. But she wasn't the only one over there. Vi and her husband. Michael, I think. Didn't want anyone else touching his drink."

"Why not?"

"He's particular. He liked to make his own."

"Do you think he suspected something?"

Paddy shook his head. "It seemed natural at the time. I didn't think anything of it. Not out of character for Michael.

Or for Richard either, for that matter. He liked to mix his own."

"And *did* he mix his own? Or did Vi or Fiona mix it?"

"Vi… I think it was Vi. She said that she had learned to make G&T just the way Richard liked it, and I'm pretty sure he let her make it for him. There was a lot of other stuff going on at the same time," he explained. "Lots of conversation, people dishing up food, in the middle of a busy park. It wasn't quiet, just one person doing one thing at a time."

Margie nodded understandingly. Even with her own little group, she would be hard-pressed to say who had eaten what, who had handled each of the drink containers, and who had helped Moushoom throughout the day. The O'Connor family picnic had been much larger and more chaotic.

Whoever had poisoned Richard had been careful. They had not wanted to poison everybody else. They wanted it to look like he'd simply had a heart attack or an accident. Maybe they thought he'd collapse at the picnic and be rushed by ambulance to the hospital. If he had been treated by a doctor at the hospital for a heart attack, there wouldn't be an automatic referral to OCME. Only if the doctor thought something needed to be investigated further. If he had thought it was a heart attack, he could just sign a death certificate to that effect, and his remains would be released directly to the family.

There would have been no investigation.

The killer would have gotten away scot-free.

"I need you to think carefully about everyone who might have handled the drinks," she told Paddy. "And was there anything else that only Richard ate or drank?"

"There wasn't anything else that was just Richard's. But if the poison could have been added to his cup or plate…"

Margie imagined the pills could have been crushed or dissolved so they could be mixed with food or drink.

"Could someone have handled his coffee or dishes?"

"Yes… maybe his coffee. Again, it is bitter. The strong taste would help to disguise the taste of the poison. Though I would think Richard would have noticed it. But anything else that we ate… I would think it would be too bland or sweet to hide a strong-tasting poison. Unless, of course, they managed to find one of those flavorless, odorless poisons they use in the movies."

"I'll need to find out more about it," Margie admitted. "But let's assume for now that it was in the tonic water or coffee…"

Paddy nodded. "Brenda and I were never at the drinks table. I don't think Helen was either. You were told about her? Helen Chang?"

"The family friend?" Margie flipped back her notes, nodding. "Yes, I think Michael mentioned her."

"I think she was like us; just let Vi or Fiona serve the drinks."

"Were their spouses with them at the table? Some of the time? All of the time?"

"Vi is divorced. Her husband was not there. Her son Ryan was there with his girlfriend, but they didn't hang out with her at the drinks table. I think they might have brought their own beer. One of those microbreweries that people get so excited about. They seem to be popping up everywhere these days."

Margie nodded. "Yes, Calgary seems to have quite a few of them."

"Ryan is actually a bartender, if I remember right," Paddy offered. "So it's not surprising that they're a little stuck up in their tastes. You spend enough time behind the counter and you start to develop opinions on what is good quality and what is just 'what everyone is drinking now.' Separating out the trendy from the good stuff."

"He's a bartender, and no one imposed on him to make anything special? Or to take a shift at the drinks table?"

"No. He made it clear from the start that he was off duty and would not be mixing any drinks."

Margie pondered on that for a moment. Was there anything that could be suspicious behavior? Was he trying to distance himself from the act and give himself an alibi? He could have brought an extra bottle of tonic water and swapped it with Vi's when no one was looking, or murmured to her that this was the good stuff.

"And he brought his own beer? Anything else?"

"I didn't inventory what he and his girlfriend brought with them. They had a cooler. Full of bottles. Everyone had a cooler. There were heaps of food and drink. People brought stuff they had made, stuff they had bought, stuff that they had bought and put into their own containers to pretend they had made it…" Paddy laughed.

Brenda allowed a smile and nod as well, confirming his observation.

Margie rubbed her temple, thinking about it. She had been there. She had been just a few meters away from the O'Connors' gathering. Paddy made it sound like it had been chaos, but that wasn't what she remembered. The various offerings had been placed on the tables so people could help themselves. There had been a separate table for the alcohol, not right beside the table with the food and drinks that the kids could help themselves to.

"Who did the children belong to? I noticed there were a few there," Margie commented.

"Oh. Not too many great-grands yet. The only ones are Michael's grandkids. His daughter Emma's. They have two—no, three, I think. Three little ones. The youngest is just a baby."

No one would want poison around them. No one would

want them to be anywhere near it. But that wouldn't be a problem if it was in the alcohol or the coffee.

"What is it you do now?" Margie asked Paddy. "You're retired. Does that mean you spend your days in the garden, or what?"

"Well, I may be retired, but I'm not dead. I went into private practice."

"Security?"

"Investigation."

"You're a private investigator?"

Paddy nodded. "At your service. Keeping my skills sharp."

"What do you investigate? Do you have a specialty?"

"A bit of this and a bit of that. Not enough to specialize in any one thing. Insurance claims, marital infidelity, fraud, you name it."

"Interesting. I don't suppose you have investigated anyone in the family for Richard?"

Paddy drummed his fingers on the table. Brenda was shaking her head, but when Paddy didn't answer immediately, she looked at him, her eyebrows going up in a query.

"Paddy, you haven't…?"

He grimaced. Brenda blinked at him.

"Paddy? Why would you? You wouldn't investigate someone in the family."

"Richard was very careful," Paddy said slowly. "When I was on the job, he would have me look into people. Make sure that everything was on the up-and-up. *Not* improper use of police systems," he told Margie. "There was always a good reason for it. And when I retired, and still planned to keep my hand in on the private side, he gave me the occasional job."

"The occasional job. Doing what?" Brenda demanded. "Looking into his business associates? Corporate espionage?"

Paddy shook his head and shifted in his seat like a child facing the teacher when he hadn't done his homework. "No. Family jobs. I didn't ever discuss them with you because it might have been awkward. I didn't want you to feel like you had something to hide from your nieces and nephews. You wouldn't want to know anything about what I was looking into, so I didn't tell you about it."

Brenda's expression had shifted, her mouth twisting into a sour knot. "You knew I wouldn't like it," she told him. "I wouldn't let you dig into the lives of my family members! You knew I wouldn't countenance such a thing."

"Richard was your brother-in-law. It wasn't like I was doing it for a stranger. He just wanted to protect his family and their assets."

"Money, you mean. It was all about money. You didn't want anyone new coming into the family who might... devalue it." Her face was dusky red and thunderous. Margie had only seen her as a nice old lady at the picnic and when she had arrived at the police station. Now, she reconsidered. There was some steel in this woman, and her words indicated that she didn't have any doubt that she could control her ex-cop husband and veto his decisions.

"Honey," Paddy held his hands up defensively. "It wasn't like that. It wasn't hurting anyone. Just protecting his family. Your family."

"By digging up dirt on them. Finding out everyone's secrets and faults. So that Richard could control them."

Paddy folded his hands together on the table and stared down at them. Margie couldn't help feeling sorry for him. He had been doing what he thought was right, helping out a family member, doing background checks for him the way he always had.

But he had kept it from Brenda, which meant he was fully aware of the fact that she would not approve. As she had suggested, he knew she would have put a stop to it if she was aware of what he was doing. He had known that she wouldn't like it and had done it anyway.

"So... what secrets do you know about the family members that I need to know?" she asked Paddy.

"I…" He looked at Brenda. "I'm going to exercise my right to remain silent. I know I'm just a witness, I have not been put under arrest, but I think I'd better stop here. I don't want to violate the privacy of the family members."

Brenda gave a single nod of agreement. Margie looked back and forth between them, hoping for a crack that she could exploit. But Paddy, in the doghouse, was not going to negotiate with her. Especially not in front of his wife.

Margie should have insisted that they be interviewed separately. She had thought, after all that had happened, that she would get more out of the old couple if she allowed them to come in together and lean on each other for support.

That had been a misjudgment.

Paddy swallowed. "I think we're done here, Detective." He rose to his feet. He held his hand out for Brenda, and she took it and stood up as well.

"I'm sorry we couldn't be more help," Brenda told Margie. "I hope you understand that we are not here to expose all of the family secrets. People deserve their privacy."

"Someone killed your brother-in-law."

"And he killed my sister," Brenda returned evenly. "I can't say I'm sorry."

CHAPTER TWELVE

*M*argie was stunned. Paddy made a gasping, groaning noise. "Brenda!"

Brenda glared at both of them.

"It may not be anything that the police would ever prosecute," Brenda said. "But you can't tell me that the way he treated her didn't have anything to do with the way she died. The doctors and police may not be able to draw a line from emotional abuse and heartbreak to her death, but I can. I will always blame him for what happened to my sister. When I go to something like this picnic, it is not because of Richard. It is for my nieces and nephews. The ones that *did* treat Evelyn right. I didn't say anything to Richard because she wouldn't have wanted me to." Her lips pressed tightly for a few more seconds before parting once more to allow a few more words to escape. "But I am not going to pretend to be sad that he is dead."

Paddy said nothing more. He took his wife's arm and looked at Margie apologetically before walking out with her.

Jones came over to stand next to Margie and watch the

couple leave before turning to her to give her an update on her progress.

"Nice little old couple," she commented with a smile.

Margie chuckled. "He is a retired police detective. His picture is on our wall. And his wife is a piece of work."

Jones's eyes widened. "Really? Well, with some people, you can never tell!"

Margie shook her head. "I did not see that one coming. She would make a good suspect if her alibi doesn't hold up. She and hubby say that they were never close to the drinks, which, according to him, is the most likely delivery mechanism for the poison."

"What do you think? Do you think it was the drinks?"

"Probably. So far. Paddy has some good points. It would be the easiest thing to poison. Several people were playing bartender or walking drinks about. One of his children brought gin and tonic specifically for him. No one else was drinking them. Nice and bitter, to mask the taste of the medication. Or else the coffee, which could be dosed individually when no one was looking."

"Sounds logical. We will have to see what everybody else says about what he ate and drank and who touched it."

"Yes," Margie agreed. "And test cups if we can. No shortcuts."

"Okay, so…" Jones pulled out her notepad to give Margie a run-down on the people she had called. "Some resistance from people who didn't want to have to come in, but almost everyone agreed to come in anyway. But I can't reach one of the sons." She looked at her notebook. "One of the middle children. David. The others all say I have the right number, but there is no answer."

"He could be in a meeting."

"They say he is an artist. And not the commercial kind. Works out of his apartment and hasn't really sold anything."

"Maybe he's on a retreat. Or has his phone turned off."

Jones nodded her agreement. "Sure. But you wanted to check in on anyone who didn't respond to my calls."

"Right." Margie looked at her watch. "I don't have any more interviews scheduled for a couple of hours, and I could use a break from this place. You want to go knock on his door?"

"Sure. Faster than sending a couple of patrol officers out to peek in windows."

They gathered their things together and headed out in Detective Jones's car to see if they could make contact with David O'Connor. It did not take long to reach his address in Crescent Heights, not a particularly cheap part of the city. Margie had not expected to find a noncommercial artist who didn't sell very much work to be living in that neighborhood. But he didn't live by himself; maybe his roommate made more and could afford the rent or mortgage payments.

Margie rang the doorbell and stood to the side, doing her best to see through the blinds in the front window whether anyone was home. She didn't see anyone approach the door. Margie reached over and rapped hard on the door.

"David O'Connor! Calgary Police. Please come to the door," she projected her voice the best she could to make sure he would be able to hear it anywhere in the house.

They waited for a while. Margie beat on the door and repeated the call. With a nod, Jones headed to the back door to see if she could see or hear anything from there. While she was in the back of the little house, there was a click, and the door opened a crack.

"Calgary Police," Margie announced again, holding her ID close to the crack for him to see. The door opened a little more, and she saw his shadowed face. "David O'Connor?" Margie asked.

"What's this about?" he asked in a small voice.

"Your father's death. Can we please come in to talk to you?"

He hemmed and hawed for a moment before finally pulling the door the rest of the way. Detective Jones returned from the back, and she and Margie strolled in after David.

CHAPTER THIRTEEN

The living room was dark because the blinds were drawn. The furniture was thrift store, not up to the quality of the house itself. A sign that they couldn't actually afford what they were paying. David's hand hovered near the lamp momentarily, indecision flickering across his face.

"Come on," Margie encouraged, "let's throw a little light on the subject."

He looked at the drawn blinds. "But…"

"They're closed. You could open them and let a little sunshine in."

"No!"

He shifted his feet and stood between Margie and the blinds, clearly not wanting her to ignore his request and open the blinds.

Hiding from someone? She didn't think he was sensitive to the sun, or he wouldn't have been at the picnic the day before. She couldn't see an artist working in the dark, though. There must be another room with bright lights on so that he could do his work.

"Do you want to meet somewhere else?" she asked.

"No. No, right here is good. I don't want to have to go anywhere else."

He eventually decided to turn the lamp on. Margie studied him, half-expecting to see that he had a black eye or other injury he was trying to keep them from seeing. But he looked just fine. Just like he had the day before.

"David, my name is Detective Patenaude. Or Detective Pat, if you like. I recognize you from yesterday. Your family and mine were in adjacent picnic areas."

He frowned at her, looking puzzled by this assertion. "Sorry, I didn't notice anyone else at the park yesterday. Were you?"

"Yes. That's fine. You were occupied with your family. You had a lot of people to visit with. Did you enjoy yourself?"

"Yeah, sure. It was nice to see everyone again."

He didn't look happy about it. But Margie didn't expect him to, when his father had died shortly after that picnic. That definitely cast a pall over the memory of the picnic.

"I'm sorry to have to intrude on you here. You did not answer your phone."

"No... I didn't feel like talking to anyone."

Margie looked around. "You don't have anyone here to keep you company? I would think that you might want family and friends around you after something like this."

"Carlos went to work. He wants to be able to take the time off for the funeral, and he doesn't know how his company is going to be about compassionate leave."

"He could take a vacation day, at least, if he doesn't qualify for compassionate leave."

"He does. At least, he should. But some companies give you a hard time. With same-sex partners, I mean. It shouldn't be any different, but people do discriminate."

"Oh," Margie nodded, suddenly getting it. If anyone

understood outdated institutional biases, it was Margie. "Well, I see how he would need to be at work today, then. But you could be with someone else in your family. Your brother and sisters. Family friends. People who understand your loss."

David went to the window and using two fingers to pry a couple of blinds apart to take a quick look outside before turning his attention back to Margie and Jones.

"So why are you here? To tell me that I shouldn't be alone? I have work to do, you know. The world doesn't stop just because Dad died. He'd be the first one to tell me to buckle up and get back to it. You can't let feelings get in the way of the real work."

"Rub some dirt in it and walk it off," Margie suggested.

David gave a bitter chuckle. "Exactly. You have a dad like that too?"

"No."

Margie let her answer stand by itself for a few long seconds, letting it sink in. Reminding him that there were worse things than a rich daddy who didn't take the time to validate his feelings. She pulled out her notebook and flipped it open.

"Were you and your partner both at the picnic?"

"Yes. Both of us were there."

"And I didn't catch his name. Carlos...?"

"Carlos Alvarez."

Margie jotted it down. "And how did Carlos feel about the picnic? Did he enjoy it?"

"How do you think it would feel to be a butterfly pinned to a display board? He feels like... it doesn't matter what he says or does; he will never fit in with my family. And he's right. They are never going to welcome someone like him into the family."

"Because he is gay or because he is Hispanic?" Jones asked.

David stared at her, waiting for her to get flustered and be embarrassed about her question.

But it was exactly the question that needed to be asked at that point, so Margie was glad Jones hadn't shied away from it. While it might be an indelicate question, it didn't help to beat around the bush or to assume she understood what David meant.

"Both," David said finally. "No reason they can't discriminate for more than one reason."

"And was that because of your father's attitude?" Margie asked.

"I guess so. I mean, he didn't get it from one of the others. He was the head of the family, the patriarch, so they adopted his attitude." He shook his head angrily. "But they didn't have to! I didn't. No one *had* to take on his ignorant prejudices. They should have fought back against them when he was being unfair."

"Of course," Margie agreed. "Each generation should be more fair and compassionate than the last. But unfortunately.... there are certain people who are determined to perpetuate those old feelings and prejudices. Trust me, I've seen it."

David shrugged and looked down at his feet. He turned slightly and looked out the window again. Margie thought about how long it had taken him to come to the door and finally open it.

"Are you expecting someone?"

"No," David said instantly. He turned back away from the window.

"It seems like you are. And... that it is someone you are afraid of."

David didn't say anything.

"Maybe it is something you should tell us about."

"Like I want to bring the police into this," he grumbled.

Margie looked at Jones, and they both just sat there for a few minutes, waiting for him to break. If this expected visit had kept him from answering the phone or the door, curled up in some safe room with a blanket over his head, it likely wouldn't take long for him to break down and tell them exactly what it was.

David fidgeted. He looked out the window and back again. He put his hands into his pockets and took them back out.

"Just what are you here for?" he demanded. "I have work to do, you know. Just because I'm a creative, that doesn't mean I just sit around on my hands all day. I have work to do."

"I just thought you were going to tell us what it is that's bothering you so much. Then we can talk about your dad and what happened to him."

"I don't want to talk to you about anything. Dad died out there kayaking. That's exactly how he would have wanted to go, so I shouldn't feel bad about it. He lived a long life. He'd achieved everything he wanted to. What is there to talk about?"

"He didn't just have a heart attack while he was out paddling," Margie told him. She cocked her head slightly. "He was poisoned at the picnic, David."

He had been distractedly looking at the window again. He looked back at Margie, startled. "What?"

"I think you heard what I said."

"Poisoned? What are you talking about? How could he have been poisoned? No one else felt sick."

"Not food poisoning. Not something that everyone else got. Your father was deliberately poisoned."

"Someone wanted to kill him?"

"Yes."

David seemed flabbergasted with the idea, despite the resentment he'd expressed only moments before. "Who?"

"That's part of the conversation we hope to have with you. We'd like your input on who you think it might have been."

"Not me," David shook his head. "I didn't want to be around the guy, but I didn't have any reason to want to kill him. In fact, it could make things more difficult for me. What are the terms of his will?"

"You don't know?"

"No. Do you?"

That was information Margie didn't have yet. She assumed that Richard O'Connor's estate would be divided among his children. Maybe with some assets set aside for friends or people he hoped to impress.

But she wouldn't know that until she found out who his estates lawyer was and got the information from him, or until the will was probated, if they couldn't get the details from anyone.

David's expression was suddenly more cheerful.

"It won't all go to Michael, will it? It will go to all of us. It isn't like in the old days, where only the oldest got something and he had to either take care of everyone else or they had to make their own way in the world, penniless."

"No, most people divide it evenly between their children," Margie agreed. "And with the size of your father's estate, I suspect that could be a sizable amount."

"Yes," David said eagerly. He didn't immediately say he would use it to pay off the mortgage or get new furniture for the house. He looked toward the blinds again, a little smugly this time.

So that was it. The person he was expecting a visit from, the person he was afraid of, would be paid off.

"Is it a loan shark?" Margie suggested.

David looked at her after a few minutes, raising his eyes to her face. "Let's just say... the kind of person who doesn't offer a flexible payment plan."

CHAPTER FOURTEEN

"So you wouldn't mind having that inheritance so you can get out of the hole," Margie suggested.

"Couldn't come at a better time," David said. He fidgeted, running his thumbnail under each of the nails on his opposite hand. Margie imagined that if he was a painter, he probably had paint under his nails all the time. She always wondered how she got so much dirt under her nails when she mostly worked on the computer or talked to people. It wasn't like she was out digging in the garden. Yet she was constantly having to clean her nails.

"But how long will it take?" David asked. "They have to read the will and do the probate and all that, don't they? I remember Mom's took a long time and she didn't have much. But maybe I could get an advance. Sometimes, they do that; they give an advance and hold the rest back for taxes and everything. Then you get another payout later, when it is all calculated out."

"It can take a while," Margie agreed. "You might need to ask the executor about that advance. Do you know who the executor is? Did he have a lawyer who handled that kind of thing?"

"I don't know. It's probably Michael. He gave Michael a lot of responsibility. Gave him the family business and everything, you know. The rest of us only hold non-voting shares."

"So you don't get input into whether or not he sells the company?"

"Sells the company? He couldn't do that. Dad wouldn't have wanted that."

"You didn't know Michael was thinking about it?"

"Thinking about what?"

Margie stared at David, trying to connect with him to be sure he was listening this time and the conversation wouldn't go completely off the rails.

"You didn't know that Michael was thinking of selling the company? He said that he didn't need anyone else's permission."

"Yes, he does!" David's voice rose. He swore. "I can't believe he's trying to sell it out from under us! We may only hold non-voting shares, but he still has to get our consent before he can sell the company or all of its assets." His eyes bored into Margie's. "That's the law. I know my rights."

"It's good that you know it. You should probably talk to Michael about it before he gets too deeply into discussions with a purchaser. I don't know what stage he's at. He might just be thinking about it at this point. I might be speaking out of turn."

"Sneaky so-and-so," David muttered. "You'd better believe I'm going to talk to him about it."

"Maybe that would get you some money," Jones pointed out. "If he sells the company and you hold shares, you will all get a portion of that, won't you?"

"Yes, but we need to vet the deal. What if Michael is just

getting a promise to pay? What if there is no cash until five or ten years down the line? I don't want to wait that long." He turned and looked out through the blinds again. "I need it now."

"We came here to talk to you about your father's murder," Margie reminded David. "Do you think we could talk about that for a few minutes?"

"I didn't have anything to do with it. I didn't even know Dad was poisoned. I thought he had trouble when he was kayaking. He was too old to still be doing that. But he didn't seem to think he needed to slow down."

"Someone at that picnic slipped him the poison," Margie said slowly. "It was done right in front of the rest of you. I want you to think back to the picnic and what you might have seen or heard. What was your father eating and drinking? Who handled his food or could have tampered with it? Someone managed to poison him, leaving the rest of you unaffected. So he ate something that the rest of you didn't, or someone passed him something where only his portion had been poisoned."

David considered this. His mental processes were considerably slower than those of his Uncle Paddy. Or he wasn't used to thinking that way. These were people he had grown up with. Or people he had been going to family events with for thirty years.

"I guess… he had his G&T's, for one thing," David said slowly. "No one else can stand them. I'm a beer man myself. Whatever you've got, I don't even care if it is a brand name. Just a can or a bottle out of the cooler. I have uncomplicated tastes."

His own way of rebelling against his father and brother. He couldn't do anything to really tick him off, or he ran the risk of not being able to get money when he needed to or being disinherited. His financial problems were probably not new. More than likely, he had a problem with gambling or spending that went back decades. There was a reason Richard had given the company to Michael. A reason he had thought that David and the girls should not have a say in anything.

"Was the gin and tonic the only thing your father consumed that no one else had?"

"Uh… I guess so. I don't know. I didn't watch everything he and everyone else ate."

"Was he dishing up his own food, or did anyone bring something over to him? If this was his party, was everyone else there to serve him and he just sat and others brought it to him?"

"No. Dad didn't just sit around. He was moving around, telling everyone he's not an invalid. Just because he was old, that didn't mean he was feeble…" David shrugged. "He says it all the time. Said, I mean."

"Were the drinks the only way someone could have poisoned him?"

"I would think so… I don't know for sure. I wasn't watching him all day."

"And who provided the gin and tonic?"

"Vi." David's face changed, and he shook his head. "Vi wouldn't have done anything to hurt Dad. If someone poisoned him, it wasn't her. She always did what Dad said. Do you know she went into law because he told her she should? I don't think he pushed her into it—he just said once that she should go into it, so she did."

"What kind of law?"

"General practice. Not like a courtroom lawyer or anything." David looked thoughtful. "I wonder if she has the will. He could have appointed *her* his executor. I didn't even think of that."

"Who was your mother's executor? Couples often write

their wills at the same time and they are set up to be mirrors of each other."

"I doubt if they wrote theirs that way. And Dad redid his after Mom died anyway. I remember that."

"But you don't remember the terms."

"I didn't know the terms. Why would he tell me that? He was a private person. He did his own thing, didn't care what other people thought about it."

"He wouldn't let you know that you would get a portion? Or a certain gift? Or that you needed to help administer a trust to pay out the grandkids?"

David just kept shaking his head. "No. He never told me or asked me about any of that stuff."

"Okay." Margie fished a business card out of her pocket. "Would you please tell me if you think of anything? Sometimes, something pops up later that you realize might be important. The way someone looked, something they were trying to hide, being in the wrong place or doing something out of character." Margie shrugged. "There could be all kinds of things. You have an artist's eye, so maybe you caught something no one else did."

David reached for the business card, then froze. His face transformed. He would not have made a good poker player. He had remembered something, and he couldn't cover it up. He turned away to look out the window again, but this time it wasn't because he was worried someone was rolling up on the house, but to hide his expression from her.

"What is it?" Margie asked. "What did you see?"

He flapped his hand at her, not turning back. "Nothing. Thanks. I've got your card in case something comes up. Just leave it on the table there."

Margie put her card down on the coffee table, which was a jumble of magazines, tissues, and sketches. Chances were, he would never see it again.

"David…"

"Just go," he told her. "I can't help you with anything. I don't know who would have poisoned my father. He wasn't the nicest guy, but people don't poison someone just because he is self-centered."

CHAPTER FIFTEEN

*M*argie checked the time as they left David's house.

"I still have a bit of time before Vi comes in for her interview. Did you have any luck getting Helen Chang, The psychiatrist?"

"Yes." Jones patted the notebook in her pocket but didn't need to take it out to refresh her memory. "She said that you could come by her office and she would make a few minutes for you, but that she was not able to take time out of her day to come and see you."

"Perfect. Let's go over there and get those few minutes. If she can't see us or give me enough time, I'll push her to come in."

Jones agreed. Once in the car, she looked up the address for the psychiatrist's office and used her phone GPS to navigate. It was in Kensington and there were no parking spaces close by, so Jones used a loading zone and relied on the police tag hanging from her rearview mirror to keep her from being towed. They had to be buzzed in at the street-level entrance, and when they reached the third floor, a receptionist welcomed them and listened to Margie's explanation of why they were there.

"Dr. Chang should finish this appointment in five minutes. Then she has fifteen minutes before her next one."

"I guess we'll see how much we can cover during that time."

"If you would like to have a seat. There is coffee available in the client service area," the receptionist pointed to a counter with a coffee machine and neatly assembled mugs. "Hot water for tea. Cold water or juice in the fridge below."

"Great, thanks."

Margie and Jones helped themselves to coffee, which smelled fresh and rich, and sat down to review their notes while waiting for the doctor.

Helen Chang ended her session promptly, and the receptionist introduced Margie to her. Chang was an Asian woman of about Margie's height with gray starting to creep into her hair, but not a crease or wrinkle on her flawless amber skin. She smiled at them politely, betraying no emotional reaction to their presence.

"Come with me," Chang said, looking at her watch. "We'll have a few minutes. I'm sure we won't need very long."

They followed her into a richly appointed office. Big rosewood desk, thick carpet, and paintings on the wall that Margie probably should be able to identify by their style. Certificates and recognition plaques prominently displayed. Margie and Jones settled into the soft visitor chairs.

"This is very nice."

"Thank you. I'm sure you want to jump right into this, so let's dispense with the small talk. How can I help you?"

"First of all… what was your role at the picnic? Were you just there as a friend of Mr. O'Connor's? Or were you there in a professional capacity? Maybe to observe someone or mediate a discussion?"

"Just as a friend."

"You were the only person there who was not a family member. Or a partner of one of the family members."

Chang considered this. "I suppose I was," she agreed.

"Was there a reason Richard wanted you there?"

"I have been a close friend of the family for years. I have counseled a number of the members at one time or the other. I guess he thought of me as family."

"He didn't want you to talk to someone in particular? Or to keep an eye on something?"

"No. I was just there for a picnic, detective."

"Did you ever provide professional services to Richard O'Connor? At any time in the past?"

"Not to him personally, no. He did hire me to counsel family members. But in that case, my oath of privacy is to the person I counseled with, not the person who paid the bill."

Margie nodded. It would not be easy to get any information from the doctor about any individual.

"Did you know of any reason anyone in the family might have to kill Richard?"

"Kill him?" Chang's eyes widened. "Certainly not."

"Mr. O'Connor was poisoned," Jones contributed. "Somebody you sat down at the table with is a murderer."

Chang shook her head in disbelief.

"You must be mistaken," she insisted. "That is not possible. No one in that family is violent. They had all been raised to respect and obey Richard, and I never knew them to behave otherwise. Murdered! That can't be true."

None of them had ever disobeyed their father? Margie knew that was not true. David, with his choice of profession, partner, and debts. Michael, planning to sell the family business without anyone else's leave. She didn't know what rebellion the girls might have shown, but there was bound to be something, especially once they were no longer living with their parents. People started their own lives, did their own things, their choices no longer dictated by a parent.

"He was given an overdose of a TCA," Jones advised. "Do you know what that is?"

"Of course I know what that is," Chang snapped. "I am a psychiatrist. I prescribe antidepressants."

"Have you ever prescribed antidepressants for members of the O'Connor family?"

"That isn't something I can discuss."

"Specifically a TCA?" Margie asked. "I think SSRIs are the usual prescription these days, aren't they?"

Chang considered her answer. "I can't tell you whether anyone in the family is on a TCA," she said, her lips barely moving, as if she could avoid breaching her patients' privacy if she didn't actually move her mouth. "But some people don't respond to SSRIs. It all depends on their own metabolism and genome. TCAs provide better relief of insomnia, OCD, chronic pain, and other specific symptoms."

Margie watched Chang's face as she spoke. She was good at masking her emotions after the initial shock of being told that Richard O'Connor had been murdered, but she still had tells. If Margie watched her very carefully, she could read some of the fleeting emotions that passed over Chang's face.

"If a person's reaction to SSRIs and TCAs can be genetic, then is it possible that several different people in a family could be on the same antidepressant?"

"Of course." Chang gave a little shrug and licked her lips, trying to decide whether to expound on this fact further or not. "If one family member responded well to a certain drug or classification of drugs, then that would probably be the first one that I tried on another family member. We can do some genetic testing now to see whether the person is more likely to respond to a particular class of drugs, but the science is still in its infancy and we are not always right."

"So a father and son, siblings, or more distant relations might share the need for the same prescription?"

Chang again shrugged, holding up her palms in a surrendering gesture. "Of course. Or they might not respond the same way at all. There is no guarantee."

"How many people in the O'Connor family have ever been on TCAs?"

"You know I can't answer that."

"I'm not asking for names. We will get subpoenas for that information if we can. I'm just asking for numbers. Is it possible that more than one person at the picnic has been on TCAs at some time?"

"It is possible, of course."

"And none of them have ever talked about doing anything violent towards Richard? Ever? Not even something that you brushed off as being flippant?"

Chang started rifling through a desk drawer. Margie watched her, wondering if she was looking for something or just trying to appear as if she hadn't heard Margie's question.

"I'm afraid there isn't much I can do to help you, detective. I need to review some files. There are exceptions to privacy laws, of course. But they are narrow. If I felt a patient was a danger to someone, for example, but not if the harm had already been done. In that case, I would not be able to respond unless there was a subpoena for the information."

"But you can't tell us whose information to subpoena," Jones said wryly.

"Of course not." Chang pulled out a pad of paper and a pen and jotted down several notes to herself. Margie could not make out the information from where she was sitting. If

Chang was hoping Margie would be able to see the names she was writing down, she had failed to make the information clear enough.

"Well, we may be back when we know more, then," Margie said, keeping her eyes on Chang's hands. However, Chang did not appear to be trying to communicate anything nonverbally.

Frustration rose within her, making her muscles tighten and her heart pound harder. She could do nothing to relieve it but to breathe slowly and try to relax her body as much as possible. David knew something. Helen Chang knew something. But neither of them would or could tell her what they knew.

"What can you tell us about Violet?" Margie asked.

"Vi?" Chang underlined or struck through something in her notes. "I can't tell you anything. I thought you understood that."

"Not medical information. Just... her relationship with Richard, her personality, things you observed outside of treatment." Margie made a gesture to indicate their surroundings. "You went to family parties. That wasn't therapy. Anything that you heard or observed at a family party where you were a guest and there were other people around, none of that could be considered private."

Chang considered this, nodding. "Vi was the oldest daughter. As the oldest girl in the family, a lot of responsibilities fell on her, both as a child and as an adult when Evelyn passed away. She and her father had a difficult relationship. His expectations of her were high. She claimed that he pushed her into an unhappy marriage with Scott Smith, a friend of her father's. Richard was not happy when they divorced. She claimed that he held the divorce against her."

"So she resented her father and blamed him for her failed marriage."

Chang nodded. "It was something she had often mentioned at family get-togethers over the past few years."

"And Richard was still friends with Scott Smith."

"Richard and Scott still moved in some of the same circles. But from what I gather, Scott blamed Richard for the break-up of the marriage. He said that if Richard had stayed out of it, he and Vi would have been fine."

Margie raised her brows. That opened up the possibility that Scott had been involved, if anyone could confirm that he had been at the park or the rowing club that day. She made a note to herself.

"And what about Richard's other children? Were there a lot of resentments there?"

"I think you will find private grievances in any family you look at. Children who resent their parents' direction, think they should be given access to their inheritance early, or who hold on to hurts from childhood. They can perceive their parents as either bullies or pushovers. Money tends to magnify some of these issues, especially if one party has it and the others do not. Money can be wielded as a weapon, used to force others into submission."

Margie nodded. "The kids find their own ways to rebel. Try to build lives that are separate and different from what their parents would have wanted or dictated."

Chang nodded her agreement. "Throw a few mental health challenges into the mix, and you can end up with some... volatile situations. But I never saw any violence in the family. Only... talk. I never had any concerns about anyone's physical safety."

She looked at her watch. "And now I'm afraid I must get ready for my next appointment. It is not good for me to be late. People get very anxious."

She stood up, dismissing Margie and Detective Jones. She picked up the note she had written to herself and put it between her keyboard and her monitor, where Margie assumed it would act as a reminder to pull her files on the various O'Connor family members Margie might be able to get subpoenas for. Margie didn't think she had enough to request a subpoena for any of them yet. That would take more legwork and more interviews.

CHAPTER SIXTEEN

*M*argie checked the time again to make sure she could get back to the office in time for her interview with Violet O'Connor. She had gotten a good amount of information from Dr. Chang, despite her inability to give Margie anything that had come of her counseling sessions. Had Chang only treated the children, or had she also treated Richard or Evelyn?

"It won't hurt anything if she has to wait a few minutes for you," Jones observed.

"No," Margie knew it was true. "It might even make her more talkative. Some people get very chatty when they are under stress."

When they returned to the office, Margie checked in to make sure that Vi was there and had been shown to the interview room to wait. She peeked at the monitor showing a video feed of the room and saw Vi shifting around in her seat, restless and bored or anxious already.

"I'll just take a run to the washroom," Margie told Jones, "Then I'll check in with her."

On her way back to the interview room, Jones stopped her.

"By the way, one more thing. The backgrounds we ran on everyone? Fiona's husband has a criminal record."

Margie paused with her hand on the doorknob to the interview room. "Oh, does he really? What for?"

"Fraud."

"That's interesting... he was Richard's financial advisor. Michael was worried he might be shady."

"Sounds like he was right."

"Hmm." Margie nodded. "Well, we'll keep on top of that. Maybe he needed to cover something up. Wouldn't the family be upset if they found out Richard's accounts had been bled dry? Do we have access to Richard's banking information yet?"

"I'll follow up," Jones promised.

"Great, thanks. I'll see whether Vi knows anything." Margie's mouth was dry. She licked her lips. "Right now, she is our best suspect. She was the one who brought the gin and tonic and mixed Richard's drinks. And it sounds like she had good reason to resent her father and all he had done 'for' her over the years."

"Good luck," Jones told her.

Margie nodded.

She hoped she wouldn't need luck. A few questions to get Vi to start talking, a sympathetic ear, and hopefully, Margie would know everything she needed to within the next hour or two.

She opened the door and greeted Vi.

"Good afternoon, Mrs. Smith. Do you go by Smith? I understand you are divorced."

"Yes," Vi confirmed. "I didn't have any reason to go back to O'Connor. Smith is... common enough that people don't automatically associate me with Scott. I could be anyone."

Margie nodded as she sat down and got settled across from Vi. "Sorry to keep you waiting. I have been swamped today. As you can imagine, interviewing everyone who was at the picnic is quite the job."

Vi nodded. She was a sixtyish woman with nearly black wavy hair that looked like she had been running her fingers through it. Her cheeks were heavily rouged, making her cheekbones look sharp and severe. She had, Margie thought, seen better days.

"So you are the oldest. You were the one in charge of the picnic arrangements?"

"The one in charge of any family event," Vi sighed. "Seeing as men are not expected to manage catering or family events. That's women's work in this family."

"Oh, I see," Margie said knowingly. "But… I suspect you are probably better at it than any of the men."

"You bet I am," Vi agreed. "And I should be after the number of family events I have organized or assisted with. I was helping Mother with it when I was just eleven or twelve. A lot of training."

"Well, I guess you are the one who can answer my questions, then, aren't you? I'm surprised that Fiona didn't do it. I thought she had a catering company. I suppose you used her for the food, but there is more to organizing an event than just the food."

"Fiona has enough on her plate—ha!—without taking that on too. I just let her deal with her own events. Just asked her to help me with the cleanup."

"Ah, well, that was kind of you. I'm sure she appreciated it."

Margie remembered Fiona's remarks about Vi not trusting her to do the catering, just trash collection. She hadn't exactly been bubbling over with appreciation.

"I hope so," Vi said. "Young people today can be so ungrateful."

Fiona wasn't much younger than Vi. She was not an inexperienced teenager.

"So I assume that by now you have heard that your father's death was not an accident."

Vi's eyes widened, and she covered her mouth. "What?"

"No one mentioned it?" Margie asked. "I've mentioned it to a couple of other family members already, and expected that you would have heard through the grapevine."

"No, I hadn't heard anything," Vi said, hand still over her mouth as if to stop herself from throwing up or saying anything she shouldn't. "How could that be? Did something happen to him out on the water? I just assumed... he'd never had any problem as far as I knew."

"What kind of problem?" Margie inquired.

"I mean... with anyone else. Why would someone kill him? They were all his friends, the people who went kayaking or canoeing."

"You think it was someone else kayaking who killed him?"

"Well, who else would it be? I can't see how he could die on the water and it not be an accident, unless someone did something... hit him over the head with a paddle or something. It's insane. You hear about things like that happening but never expect it to happen in your own family."

"No." Margie shook her head. "It wasn't someone out on the water. It wasn't another kayaker. It was someone from your family, at the picnic."

Vi gave a startled laugh. "Well, that's even harder to believe," she declared. "It couldn't have been someone at the picnic. No one would do that."

"Are you on any medications, Mrs. Smith?"

Vi closed her mouth. Her brows drew together. "Medications? I don't see how that is any of your business."

"It is part of our investigation into your father's death. Were you on antidepressants?"

"No, certainly not."

"No? How about any others in your family? It's pretty common these days. It is not such a taboo as it once was. We're talking about it more. So *let's talk*." Margie gave her an encouraging smile.

"I would not share my family's private troubles with you. You don't need to know that."

"I would like to know where the killer got the tricyclic antidepressants he poisoned your father with."

"And you think they got into my medications? Someone stole my prescription and used it to poison my father? What a thought!"

"Where do you think they got it, then?"

"I have no idea." Scowling, Vi shook her head. "I'm not sure I even believe that he was poisoned. You're just trying to start something... to make this a bigger story than it is. Sensationalize it. My father had a heart attack while he was kayaking. That's all."

"He had high levels of TCA in his blood. Somebody dosed him pretty good."

Vi shook her head continually, refusing to accept it.

"The medical examiner says that it was homicide," Margie assured her. "That is what his report will say."

"He's wrong." Vi ran her fingers through her hair, tugging on it anxiously. "Maybe it was suicide," she suggested. "Homicide doesn't mean murder. He could have killed himself."

"Was he on antidepressants?"

"No. He was never sick a day in his life," Vi said automatically, as if this fact had been drilled into her for years.

"He didn't take any medications. He was healthy. Ate right. Exercised right. He took care of himself." She breathed out, and a tear glistened in one eye. "He thought he would live forever."

"Unfortunately, it doesn't matter how well you take care of yourself; you don't get to live forever," Margie said sympathetically. "No matter what you do, you reach the end sooner or later. Your father may have still had a few good years left in him if it hadn't been for this, but he wasn't going to live forever."

"Of course not," Vi said in a more natural voice. "No, of course not."

"There is nothing shameful about taking medication if you need it. Are you sure Richard wasn't taking anything else? Even if he said he wasn't? Could you be certain? Could he have been hiding it because he *was* ashamed? If other people in the family suffered from depression, it isn't much of a stretch that they had inherited it from him."

"If he was hiding it... how would I know?" Vi sniffled. "Maybe he was depressed. Maybe he decided that he'd had enough, and... he was ready to go. So he arranges for the family to get together for one more picnic in our old spot, and..."

And he took extra pills with his picnic lunch. Said goodbye to his family, and went off for one last paddle. Margie could see the possibility. It would not be easy to prove one way or the other.

Maybe that was why Vi suggested it. She knew she was the one who had brought the gin and tonic and had mixed her father's drinks. She had to know that if Richard had been poisoned, that put her at the top of the list of people who could have administered the poison.

"Why don't you tell me what happened?" Margie told Vi, as if she knew that Vi had something to confess. "You had to get the family together for another event. Your father wanted to grandstand some more. He was always telling you what to do. You were tired of it. Tired of the way he had pushed you into a loveless marriage and how he would just never stop. You could never live up to his expectations. You'd had enough. So one last farewell…"

"I would never do something like that," Vi insisted.

"You brought his favorite drink. You mixed it for him. One last chance to impress him, to show him you could do something for him, mix it the way he liked it. But with a little extra kick. Had you already mixed the TCA into the bottle of tonic water? Or was that too risky, in case someone else wanted to use the tonic water? Someone might ask Ryan to mix a cocktail for them."

"I didn't have any poison. I wouldn't poison anyone."

"Who else could have done it? You're the one who mixed Richard's drinks."

"It could have been in something else. I wasn't paying any attention to what Dad was eating. Anyone could have given it to him."

"But it would have to have been something that could be poisoned individually. They couldn't just mix it into a macaroni salad or tray of Nanaimo bars."

Margie thought she saw a quick flash of fear in Violet Smith's eyes, and then it was gone.

"I'm sure I don't know what happened," Vi said calmly. "It certainly wasn't in anything I gave him."

Margie tried to hold her gaze. Vi's eyes slid away from her.

"If it wasn't you, then who do you think was sitting around that fire who wanted your father dead? You tried to point at one of his boating friends, but I think you know it wasn't one of them. It was one of you. You or your siblings, or one of the grandkids."

"The grandkids? Why would one of them want to hurt him? He doted on his grandkids. *They* didn't have any reason to want to kill him!"

She stopped and bit her lip, realizing too late that saying the grandchildren had no reason to kill him but not saying the same about her siblings was a silent accusation of her siblings.

"He didn't push the grandkids the same way as he pushed his own children?" Margie asked. "He didn't insist that their lives had to follow the paths he'd set for them? That they needed to marry the right people? Have the right number of children?"

"He wasn't that bad," Vi protested. "He didn't dictate number of children."

"Maybe not for you," Margie said slowly, "since your children would not carry on the O'Connor family name. Only Michael's line would, since David wouldn't have any children. The only great-grandchildren were in Michael's line, weren't they?"

"The other grandchildren just didn't have any yet," Vi protested. "Michael was the oldest, so his children were the oldest. The others would have had children sooner or later. And David *could* have had children," she defended him. "They do that, now. Let gay couples adopt or use a surrogate. It isn't the same world as it was in my father's day."

"Not by a long shot," Margie agreed. She thought about her world, her mother's world, and the world Moushoom had lived in. Things had changed a lot in that time. Many things for the better.

"So you don't think it was one of the grandchildren," she prompted.

"No," Vi shook her head. "It wouldn't have been one of them."

Margie was quiet, letting Vi stew. Letting the silence

build. A picture was starting to form in her head. It was obvious that Vi was the best candidate for having given her father the poisoned drinks. But did she actually have access to TCA? They needed to find out whether she had a prescription or other source.

The other viable alternative Vi had offered was that Richard had committed suicide. There would have been no need for a clandestine poisoning. No need for the tonic water to be spiked ahead of time. No need for sleight of hand or misdirection. Richard had seemed fine when he left the picnic, but impaired when he arrived at the boathouse. How much time had passed in between? Had there been time for him to take pills after leaving the family picnic and for them to get into his bloodstream by the time he arrived to pick up his kayak?

Richard had had the opportunity, and like with Vi, Margie needed to know where he could have gotten TCA if he had intended to commit suicide.

CHAPTER SEVENTEEN

*M*argie was glad to get home at the end of the grueling day. It was good to get away from the tales of the O'Connor family, their secrets and grievances. It was sad to see how much Richard's personality and choices had messed up the family. He wasn't an abusive drunk like many of the fathers she had seen in her life and on the job. She had seen the devastation they could wreak on a family. But Richard's self-centeredness and attempts to control his children had still led to a lot of pain and dysfunction in their lives.

He seemed like he had been happy enough, living the life he did, but that probably wasn't true either. Margie often thought that money would solve a lot of her problems and make things easier, but the wealthy people that she was exposed to on the job made her wonder if a person could ever be happy with the wealth they had. It seemed to come with its own set of problems. Richard's children had grown up with a life of privilege, but what good had it done? What peace had it brought them?

They didn't have what Margie had when she returned

home at the end of the day. Christina and Stella waiting for her. Pleasant conversation, a shared meal, maybe some time in front of the TV, if she could put her work and ruminations about which of the family members might have killed Richard to the side. After a good night's sleep, maybe she would wake up in the morning with some clarity about the case. Let her subconscious brain come up with the solution.

Stella was barking her head off as Margie approached the house. And it didn't sound like her usual welcoming bark. She frowned as she turned the door handle and found it locked. While it was safer for Christina to lock the door when she was home alone, she rarely bothered to lock it after returning home from school. Margie dug her keys back out of her purse. Stella was clawing at the other side.

With anxiety growing in her stomach, Margie unlocked the door and pushed it open. She reached down to corral Stella and keep her in the house, but Stella ignored her hand and bolted past her.

"Stella!" Margie called after her. "Come back here!"

The dog didn't run far, her streak across the yard ending at the Alberta rose bush, which she watered generously. Margie knew as she pushed the door open the rest of the way that Christina wasn't home, but called out to her anyway.

"Christina? Are you here? Are you okay?"

A foul odor hung in the air. Margie gagged, covered her nose and breathed through her mouth. They were careful to make sure Stella had regular access to the backyard to avoid any accidents, and Stella was fastidious about her toilet habits. It had been a long time since they'd had a screw-up that had resulted in an accident.

It was not the warm domestic scene that Margie had pictured walking into. She put down her bag, took off her coat, and immediately went to work to get the mess cleaned up. Stella returned from the yard through the door Margie had left slightly open and nosed at Margie as she cleaned. She whined anxiously.

"I know, girl," Margie told her, pushing her away. "It's not your fault. I don't know what happened, but it isn't your fault."

Stella whined, trying to get closer to get loves and ear scratches from Margie, and Margie had to push her away firmly. "No. Sit. Stay."

Stella stayed, but continued to whine. As Margie finished, Stella looked toward the door, still hanging open, and squirmed in place, letting out a couple of barks to let Margie know she wanted to be released from the "stay" command. Margie leaned on one knee, too tired to bounce to her feet, and watched Christina enter.

Christina's expression was stormy. When she looked around, that changed. Her eyes widened and a flash of guilt appeared and was gone again in a second.

"Come here, Stella," she called to the waiting dog. Stella bounded over to her and nuzzled her, whining.

"Where were you?" Margie demanded. She got creakily to her feet, her knees protesting about the position she'd been forced into to clean up Stella's mess. "You left her to have an accident?"

"I just got here," Christina snapped. "I'm sorry, but I couldn't get home any earlier, okay?"

"No, it isn't okay. If you are going to be late or aren't going to be here for any reason, you're supposed to let Mrs. Rose know so that she can let Stella out." Margie flung a hand in the direction of the neighbor's house. "You know that! We've made arrangements to cover circumstances like this. You have responsibilities!"

"I know! I made a mistake. I was upset and I didn't think about it. Sometimes things happen, you know. It isn't the end of the world."

"No, but it is cruel to Stella. And I just had to clean up your mess at the end of a long, difficult day. This is not what I wanted to come home to."

"It isn't what I wanted to come home to, either."

Margie strode out to the bins in the back lane to dispose of the stinking evidence of Christina's neglect. She stood there for a moment, breathing in the cool evening air and trying to calm her anger and disappointment.

Christina was normally a very responsible girl. But sometimes, things happened that were beyond a teenager's control. Maybe she hadn't been able to get to her phone to let Mrs. Rose know to let Stella out. Margie didn't know yet what had happened and shouldn't fly off the handle.

CHAPTER EIGHTEEN

*I*n better control of herself, Margie returned to the house. Christina was crouched down to Stella's level, giving her hugs and apologizing for not being home. Stella was lapping up the attention and did not appear permanently traumatized by the incident. Christina looked up at Margie, covering her mouth with her hand to hide her expression.

"I'm sorry, Mom. I really am. I didn't mean to hurt Stella." She scratched Stella's ears vigorously.

"So, what happened?"

Christina didn't answer immediately. She struggled to come up with the words. Eventually, she shook her head. "Things are just all messed up. I can't get into it. I don't even know where to start."

"Are you okay?"

Christina nodded.

"Do you need help with something?"

"No. It's just personal stuff." Christina rubbed at leaky eyes with her wrists, and winced. "Ouch. Fur in my eyes." She pushed Stella away from her, rubbed her hands on her pants, and picked at her eyelashes, trying to get the hair out of her eye. "I just... I'm just sorry. I know I should have called. I was just... all wrapped up. I didn't even think about it."

Margie couldn't think of what to say. She wanted to lecture Christina on being responsible and again reproach her for not being there to care for her dog. But what good would that do? Christina already admitted culpability and had already apologized. What more could Margie ask from her? Groveling? Begging for forgiveness? Insisting on a more detailed explanation?

She could ground Christina, but what good would that do? Margie couldn't physically make her do anything, and she had friends with cars. The last thing she wanted was to send Christina running away from her, even for one day.

Margie opened her arms to Christina without a word. Christina stood up and embraced her, needing to bend over to hug Margie. "I *am* sorry, Mom."

"I know. Now I'm worried about you. Stella will be okay. She's already forgotten about it. What about you?"

Christina nodded, giving Margie another squeeze, then let go. "It will be okay," she said, wiping her eyes again.

"Is it something that happened at school? Something with Tracy?"

Christina sniffled. "Tracy," she acknowledged. "But... I think it is straightened out. I just..." Her shoulders slumped, and she looked around. "I just want to collapse and drink myself into a coma."

Margie's alarm must have shown in her expression. Christina gave a choked laugh and held her hand up. "Coke," she said. "Not booze. I could drink a whole case. And a liter of ice cream."

"Sounds like a plan," Margie agreed. She pulled out her phone. "But we're going to need pizza to go with that. We can't have that much sugar without balancing it out with fat and protein."

Christina laughed and sniffled at the same time, producing a snort. "Of course," she agreed. "I'll get the drinks."

While Margie ordered pizza, Christina got out a bottle of Coke and poured it into two glasses over cubes of ice. She poured slowly as it fizzed up, then positioned the glasses neatly on the table and got out Stella's dinner.

They sat down and sipped the drinks slowly. As much as Margie wanted the details of what had happened between Christina and Tracy, she could see that Christina wasn't ready to talk about it, and the girl deserved her privacy. Margie could give her some processing time. With all of the teenage hormones raging through her system, the littlest thing could blow up into something catastrophic.

So she filled the time talking to Christina about the O'Connor case. Nothing that would identify anyone, nothing too sordid or revealing. But it was easier to talk to her about someone else's drama and the day that Margie had been through than expecting Christina to talk about her day, even just mundane stuff about school and not her relationship problems.

"That's messed up," Christina declared with a whistle. "He was a bad dad, so one of them knocked him off?"

Margie shrugged. "I've seen people kill for a lot less. An argument over what program to watch on TV. A hit of heroin. A girl that neither one of them even cared about." Margie shook her head. "The human race can be pretty horrible to each other."

"Are you sure it was one of his kids?"

"Pretty sure," Margie said. "Not one hundred percent."

"And they aren't, like, teenagers? They are grown adults?"

"In their fifties and sixties," Margie agreed. "Certainly old enough to figure out a better way to solve their differences."

"Why would they even have to talk to him? If they're grown adults, why not just do their own thing and have nothing to do with him?"

"That would probably have been a better approach. But I think they were all afraid of losing the money. The money he gave them while he was alive, and the money they would get when he died."

Christina rolled her eyes. "Money is *not* that important," she declared.

Margie smiled. She agreed, but wondered whether Christina was showing her wisdom or naiveté on the subject.

"What do you think you would do?" she asked. "If you had the chance for financial stability and the ability to afford the things you wanted, or be free to do your own thing without having to report to someone on it? What would you choose?"

She thought about David, the one child she knew had decided to go against Richard's dictates by choosing Carlos. And about his deep financial debt and fear of the men who would come to collect the money he didn't have. Of course, the choice wasn't necessarily between David being with the one he loved or in mortal peril. He could have chosen to find a stable job instead of trying to make it as an artist, assuming he was able. Avoiding gambling or debt. But his choices had definitely put him at odds with the father who could have rescued him from the situation he was in.

Would Richard have helped him if it weren't for Carlos? Had David even asked? Or had he just assumed that the answer would be no or refused to go back to his father for anything? Or had Richard bailed him out so many times that he had refused to do it again?

Had the only remaining option David had seen been to

get his inheritance? Did he know what he would get from his father's estate? He had seemed to be pleasantly surprised at the prospect of receiving money due to his father's murder, but that could have been an act.

"Well, you would never make me make a choice like that," Christina pointed out.

Margie was glad Christina knew she would not be rejected out of hand for her choices, even if they were against what Margie would have wished for her.

"No, I wouldn't," she agreed. "I'm just saying imagine it. What do you think you would do?"

"There are a lot of ways to make money or get help," Christina said slowly. "I know it would be really hard. I know it's been hard for you as a single mom, going to school and then on a patrol cop's salary. But you made it. And I think... if I tried hard enough, I could too. I wouldn't want to give up on my dream. Whatever it was." She sighed. "It would be nice to have a dream. To know where I'm going and what I want from life."

"For some people, that's clear. But for others... I think for most of us... we're just feeling our way around in the dark. Touching one thing and then another, trying to figure out what would make us happy. And *some* people have a dream, and then when they achieve it... they find out that it doesn't make them happy and they have to go back to the beginning to figure it out. I think I'd rather work it out a bit at a time and be pretty sure that I was moving in the right direction than to go gung ho for something and then decide I didn't want it."

"Do people really do that?"

Margie thought of some of the examples she had seen of just that. "Oh, yes. People who get a law degree or doctorate and then decide that isn't what they want to do with their lives. Go on to remake themselves all over again. And I think some people just like going to school and can never quite get to finding something productive to do with their lives after they stop."

Christina made a face. "You've got to be kidding. Who would want to go to school forever?"

"I can't understand it myself," Margie admitted. "I was never big on school. But some people just keep moving from one degree to another and never settle down. I never went to university; maybe I would have felt differently about it if I had."

"So what are you going to do in the murder case? Do you know who did it, and you just need to get enough proof? Or are you still trying to figure out who did it?"

"There are a few ways I could go. I'm not sure yet." Margie yawned. "I'm hoping it will be clearer in the morning."

Christina nodded sagely. "Things are always more clear after a good sleep. You'll know what to do when you wake up."

Margie hoped that it was true.

CHAPTER NINETEEN

$\mathcal{M}$orning did not bring the perfect clarity that Margie had hoped for. Things were better organized in her mind, but her subconscious mind had not come to a brilliant conclusion in the middle of the night and provided her with the solution to O'Connor's murder.

Margie didn't have to rush in to the office, but stayed home to get Christina off to school. She had a twinge of worry in the back of her mind that with whatever problems she'd had with school and Tracy the evening before, Christina might not want to go to school in the morning and would fake sick or try some other scheme to avoid it. But Christina seemed more serene in the morning. Maybe she had achieved the clarity that Margie had been hoping for.

Christina got ready for school, kissed Stella goodbye on the muzzle and promised her that she would be back after school to let her out, no matter what, while looking at Margie to make sure that she heard. Margie wanted to lecture her about her irresponsibility the day before and emphasize how important it was for her to follow through and be there for Stella, or else to let Mrs. Rose know that she needed to come over to let Stella out.

But experience told her to leave it alone. Christina had acknowledged her mistake of the day before and had just said that it would not happen again, so what good would come from trying to make her feel bad about it? Instead, Margie hugged her daughter and saw her off to the bus without mention of incident.

She texted Sergeant MacDonald and Detective Jones to let them know that she was going to go back to the park to talk with Emily, the boathouse manager.

She decided she couldn't go to Glenmore without Stella, so she grabbed the leash and called Stella to go for a ride. Stella dashed out to the car, dancing around excitedly while she waited for Margie to open the door.

"Okay, okay, relax," Margie told her. "You like going out, don't you? We're going to go back to the park again. You had a good time there on Monday."

Stella sat on the passenger seat beside Margie, her tail thumping loudly as she watched out the window. She loved riding in the car. And she was eager to find out where Margie was taking her, sure it would be somewhere wonderful like the park or the pet store where she got treats, rather than the vet. She wasn't even bad about going to the vet when she was due for shots. She got treats and lots of attention there, too.

Margie found the location on her GPS, careful to pick the parking lot closest to the boathouse rather than on the other side of the park, proud of herself for remembering. She'd be there all day if she had to traipse from one side of the park to the other. Not that Stella would mind. And if Margie told MacDonald that she was pursuing the investigation all day, it wouldn't matter to him if she didn't show up in the office. As long as she filed reports showing her progress.

She got to the park with only one missed turn, and she was able to perform a U-turn right away to correct it. One day, she would be able to find her way around Calgary without making any wrong turns, even without the GPS.

Margie laughed at herself. *Really?* Maybe when technology reached the stage when she could have a GPS embedded directly into her brain.

With Stella on leash, Margie followed the signs to the rowing club and the boathouse. Things were pretty quiet. She let herself into the boathouse and looked around.

"Can I help you?" Emily approached her, and after looking at her for a moment in confusion, remembered who she was. She nodded in greeting. "Detective Pat. I thought... did you need something else?"

She saw Stella, and her eyes lit up. "Aw, who is this darling?"

"This is Stella."

"Hi, Stella!"

Emily reached a hand out to the dog to sniff. Stella pushed her head into Emily's hand and Emily scratched her ears. Margie smiled.

"I wanted to go through your statement with you to make sure we got everything down correctly and to find out if you had remembered anything else. And I have another question."

"Uh, sure. Nothing else came to mind. I can read through it again if you want me to, but nothing is going to be any different."

"That's fine. I want to make sure we got everything right. I guess you have probably heard by now that Mr. O'Connor's death was not an accident or a natural death."

Emily looked away from Margie, chewing on her lip, which already looked chapped and painful. "Do you really think that..." she trailed off uncertainly.

Margie gave her some time, waiting for her to finish.

"I mean... I heard some things, but I can't understand how anyone could think that it was murder. Mr. O'Connor was on his own when he got here. He had just come from his family picnic. He went out on his own... he seemed like he was okay..."

"You noticed that he was clumsy, though; you wondered whether he'd had too much to drink. You knew that he was impaired. Well, it turns out that his blood alcohol level was low. He'd only had one or two drinks in the previous few hours. But he had very high levels of something known as TCA. And that was what killed him. It caused a heart attack."

"He looked a little unstable, but he didn't look like he was going to die."

Margie nodded sympathetically. "I'm sorry you had to deal with this. You might want to talk it over with a therapist or someone to deal with trauma. Sometimes that helps."

"I didn't actually see him die, so I'm not traumatized. But... I hate to think that I let him get into his kayak when he was dying. Even if I just thought he'd been drinking a bit... I shouldn't have let him."

Margie nodded. She wouldn't get into that. Whether Emily had gone against the rules established by the club. Whether she was partially liable if she let an impaired club member into the water. Emily would have to deal with the rowing club on those issues. They might gloss over them and hope that no one in the family decided to sue. Or they might terminate her and have their insurer get involved to shore up their defenses.

"I did have another question unrelated to that."

"Yes?" Emily let out a sigh, seemingly relieved about the change of topic.

"I wondered whether Mr. O'Connor's friend, Scott Smith, was here that day."

"Mr. Smith?" Emily frowned, thinking about it. "I don't think so. Let me just check the logbook."

"I would like a copy of the log," Margie told her, surprised that this record hadn't been mentioned during her inquiries about Richard O'Connor. Maybe Emily and the management of the rowing club hadn't said anything about it because of Emily's clear recollection of Richard's arrival. There hadn't been any need to check the records.

"Oh, yeah, of course," Emily said, sweeping back her blond hair. She didn't demand to see a subpoena for the information, apparently unconcerned about client privacy.

Emily went over to her desk, tucked in one corner of the boathouse, and turned through the pages slowly.

"Yeah, he was here," she agreed. "After Mr. O'Connor."

She pointed out the line on the log, which put Scott Smith there a couple of hours after Richard, but before his body was discovered. Margie tried to imagine a scenario where Smith could be considered a suspect in the murder. She couldn't make it work. Not with the length of time that Richard had been in the water and the other details in the medical examiner's preliminary report determining the time of death. Smith had arrived after Richard was in the water. Possibly after Richard was dead. The medication needed time to do its work. It wasn't an instant death.

That in itself had made the TCA a good method to murder the man. It meant that Richard had been on his own, the family dispersed, and the picnic site cleaned up before he had absorbed enough of the drug to kill him. And, as far as she could tell, it eliminated Scott Smith from the running as the killer. Not that she'd thought he had much of a motive from the start.

Margie snapped a picture of the logbook and checked to make sure the image was clear.

"Thank you, Emily; I appreciate all of your help. I hope… you don't spend much time blaming yourself for what happened. That drug would have killed Mr. O'Connor whether he had been on water or land. It didn't make any difference. He didn't have any water in his lungs; he was dead by the time he tipped over. At least… he died doing what he loved."

Emily sniffled. "Thank you, Detective Pat. That helps."

CHAPTER TWENTY

*M*argie and Stella bid Emily goodbye and left the boathouse. Rather than return to her car, Margie looked at the trail map and found her way to the picnic sites where she and the O'Connor family had enjoyed their Victoria Day picnics. She heard children laughing and playing in a nearby playground. She sat down at the picnic table where she had sat visiting with her family and enjoying the picnic fare. She closed her eyes and pictured the family at the next site over.

A large crowd. Three generations plus a fourth comprising a few little children. A more sophisticated celebration. Alcoholic drinks and catered dishes. A few potluck items. Coolers filled with soft drinks and some other options. More than once, voices had been raised in anger and then lowered again. Margie had been concerned that things might escalate as the alcohol was consumed, but eventually, people started to disperse.

She knew their names and identities now. The ones who she hadn't interviewed directly were still on her radar. She knew their names and how they were related to the other attendees.

Richard, the patriarch, overseeing it all. Giving orders and making comments when he saw something he didn't like. His middle-aged children moving to obey him, some of them slow and others snappy. Lots of hidden resentments and aggression. Lots of subtext that Margie hadn't been able to interpret when she had been on the outside. Could she pull it all together now to reconstruct what had happened? She had the various narratives to guide her in what had happened. Who had been close to the drinks, mixing them and handing them out?

Stella nosed around the picnic area, sniffing out all the interesting smells left behind by the various visitors. She tugged Margie toward the O'Connor's picnic spot.

"What is it?" Margie asked her, letting Stella lead her. Squirrels, hot dog drippings, baby diapers—there were probably all kinds of fascinating smells to follow.

As Stella meandered across the picnic site, Margie's thoughts followed a similar random path. Vi bringing the ingredients and mixing the drink for her father. Fiona handing them out. Uncle Paddy and Aunt Brenda being waited upon. Dr. Chang… where? Each of the four siblings with their partners. Michael with his three young children.

Stella pawed at something tangled in a clump of weeds, trying to get it out. Margie bent down for a look at what it was and saw the familiar orange plastic of a prescription bottle. She took a few pictures of it in place. Then she dug a pair of gloves out of her purse and put them on, snapping them into place. She picked up the bottle by the edges and turned it to read the label.

Amitriptyline

Her heart raced. The most common TCA. She tried to picture who had been sitting closest to the bottle. Several of the women. Purses piled on the table. Jackets removed as the day heated up and they were moving around, preparing the drinks and dishing up plates for Richard and anyone else who was not prepared to get up and do it themselves.

How many times had Margie lamented the lack of pockets in women's clothing? Sleek, slim-cut outfits that would have been "ruined" by the presence of pockets and their contents. Men made fun of women for bulky, omnipresent purses. But they didn't have to figure out what to do with wallets, phones, keys, feminine hygiene items, makeup and lip balm, tissues, and whatever other items a woman needed to carry, not just for herself, but her whole family.

If the killer had found herself with the empty poison bottle in her hands and nowhere to put it because she had become separated from her purse or jacket and too many eyes were on her, what was she to do with it? Drop it and kick it into the closest ground cover?

Margie looked inside. Powdery residue coated the inside of the container. Not a light dusting left by pills rubbing the side of the container, but a thicker coating as if it had been filled with powder. Pills ground down so the poison could more easily be dissolved in a drink.

Margie looked again at the prescription label, skimming over the dosage instructions to find the patient's name.

Ambrose White

Margie's mind whirled as she tried to figure out how the name connected with everything else. *Who the heck was Ambrose White?*

She knew the bottle was evidence of the poisoning. There was no way it was a coincidence that an emptied bottle of Amitriptyline had been left a few feet away from where Richard's fatal drink had been prepared.

It didn't make any sense until her eyes drifted to the name of the prescribing physician.

Dr. H. Chang

Not a family member who had used their own prescription to poison Richard, but someone who could issue a prescription to another patient, real or fake, and then fill it for her own purposes.

But why?

Stella barked and strained on the leash, nearly pulling Margie over with a sudden lunge.

"Whoa, whoa, Stella," Margie protested automatically, pulling back.

Looking up, she saw the other woman approaching. Not Dr. Chang, but the severe-looking Violet. She scowled at Margie, looking at the bottle in her hand. "Why did you come back here?" she demanded.

"I had more questions," Margie said. She kept her voice steady and firm, not allowing emotion to enter it. "More questions about what happened here on Monday. Stay where you are, please." She didn't want Vi getting any closer to her. She might be a senior, but she appeared to be in good shape, and Margie did not want this to turn into a physical confrontation. She had been going for a walk in a local park with her dog; she had not brought her gun or handcuffs with her.

"You shouldn't be here," Vi said tightly. "Everybody has cooperated with you and answered your questions. Why would you come back here?"

"Why did you come back here?" Margie asked. She held up the bottle. "To get this? Why bother, if it didn't have your name on it? I suppose you handled it without any gloves. People would have questioned why you were wearing gloves while mixing drinks, even post-COVID."

"Fiona was supposed to clean everything up," Vi said

tightly. "She was supposed to make sure that nothing was left behind, but when I asked her if she had seen the pill bottle Helen had lost, she said she hadn't come across it." She shook her head. "She thought she should have been allowed to cater the whole event, when she couldn't even manage the cleanup? She was always spoiled. Baby of the family. Never learned the value of work."

"You and Dr. Chang were both in on it together?" Margie asked, watching Vi for any sign of a threat.

"In on what?" Vi asked, not about to confess to anything, even if it was clear that she had played a part here. She could point to Chang and say that it had been her. Chang's name was on the prescription. Vi could have handled the bottle innocently, picking it up after Chang had dropped it. Touching it was not proof of her involvement.

"Why would Dr. Chang want to kill Richard?" Margie shook her head. "I don't see a motive for her. Only if she was helping someone else. But… why?"

It didn't make sense for Helen Chang to help with the murder. She knew many of the family secrets, but even so, therapists were often aware of terrible abuse their clients had suffered and did not attempt to balance the scales or get vengeance for what had been done. And from all of the interviews Margie had conducted, she had not found a trend of terrible abuses by Richard. People with hurt feelings, yes; people who had gotten tired of dealing with a hard, self-centered man, but not anyone who had suffered real trauma or abuse.

"Why don't you ask her yourself?" Vi asked.

Margie glanced around, scanning the trees and trying to see around any obstacles to see if they were alone or if Chang was there herself, ready to help out with whatever Vi had in mind. They were there to clean up, to make sure that no one could put together what they had done. They had not expected to find Margie there. There was no reason to think that they were prepared to do violence.

Stella barked loudly at Vi, then whirled around to find Helen Chang approaching from the other direction, attempting to pincer Margie between them. Margie didn't see any weapons, and both were older women, presumably not trained in martial arts or hand-to-hand combat.

Margie backed up to prevent Chang from being able to approach her unseen. Stella growled deep in her throat. A sound that was much more menacing than her bark. Margie looked down at Stella and followed her gaze. Behind them. Someone else in the trees. Margie couldn't see or hear who it was, but Stella could. Someone who was a more significant threat than the two women.

"Who is there?" Margie demanded, using her tough cop voice. "Show yourself. Come out where I can see you with your hands behind your head."

There was no movement that Margie could see from the trees. The two women didn't give any indication that they knew who else was there, which suggested to Margie that they knew exactly what was going on. They didn't need to ask questions or look bewildered. They were not surprised or confused by the presence of a third person.

Margie decided it was time to move. She was a cop, and she had a good strong voice and good self-defense skills, but trying to fight three parties without a weapon or handcuffs, when she had no idea of the third person's physical attributes or weapons, was not a good idea.

She pulled on the leash. "This way, Stella," she murmured.

Stella initially resisted, wanting to go after the unknown figure in the trees, but with another tug, she obeyed and she and Margie withdrew, putting some space between themselves and the three opponents. She tucked the pill bottle into a jacket pocket to free up one hand and pulled out her phone. She dialed 9-1-1 and held it to her ear as she withdrew, watching for any serious threat. Her whole body was tense, almost shaking from how rigidly she held herself. She knew she needed to relax if she wanted to protect herself. Being stiff as a board while fighting or fleeing was not effective.

"Officer in need of assistance," Margie barked as soon as the emergency operator answered. "Detective Margie Patenaude. North Glenmore Park." She looked for a sign identifying the picnic area or a mile marker. There were kilometers of paved trails, but she couldn't remember seeing any location markers. "Contact Detective Lewis Riley. Location is the picnic area we were at on Monday. Track my GPS location; I'll keep the call active."

She looked around herself. She was headed toward the reservoir. There might be a landing number if she got closer to the water's edge. There were numerous stairways, boat launches, and walkouts around the reservoir. They had to be identifiable somehow.

Margie walked toward the reservoir, trying to tamp down the panic that rose in her stomach at being close to a large body of water. It looked bottomless. It looked as though it went on forever.

CHAPTER TWENTY-ONE

*H*elen Chang and Vi Smith were moving toward her, closing in.

Whoever was back in the trees was also moving, but Margie couldn't yet see who it was.

She was up on a ridge, looking down at the reservoir. It was three flights of stairs down to get to the level of the water. There would be some kind of numbering on the boat landing below her, she was sure. The dispatcher was asking questions in Margie's ear, but she was busy calculating, trying to work it all out.

If she wanted her fellow law enforcement officers to be able to reach her, she needed to give an exact location. The park was huge. They might or might not be able to get Lewis. He might be undercover and they wouldn't have a way to get to him that quickly. Hopefully, they could narrow in on her phone's GPS, but it wasn't always a reliable way to locate a caller.

She didn't know whether the signal would be better or worse in the park. The cell signal was not as reliable; Margie knew that, but didn't know if the GPS signal relied on the same technology. She knew that downtown, the GPS signal could reflect off of the buildings as if she were in a cavern, and say she was somewhere other than where she really was. Would the reservoir reflect the signal the same way?

As much as she was loath to go down toward the water, she couldn't see a better strategy to give the dispatcher her exact location than finding a dock number. She might be making it easier for her pursuers to pin her down, but she thought she could still climb along the shore, through the Saskatoon berry bushes, willow, poplar, and scrub brush. There were pathways forced through the vegetation down there. Not paved pathways, but "goat trails" that people and animals exploring along the shore had used for generations. A narrow trail worn down through the years between the trees and over the rocks. She could follow one of them, avoiding pursuers until help arrived.

Fortifying herself with a deep breath, Margie started down the stairs.

Steep staircases were not her favorite thing. But they were sturdy and there was a handrail.

Children went up and down them. Elderly adults with canes or walking sticks. There was nothing to worry about.

Margie pushed herself to descend quickly, trying not to imagine the pain if she tripped and tumbled headfirst when her toe caught on a board.

Stella was panting at her side, enjoying the run, happy to go down with Margie to check out the water and maybe get a chance to chase the waterfowl that bobbed up and down near the shoreline, or maybe a fish sunning in shallow water.

The dog didn't know how dangerous the water could be. One person had already died there this week. The odds of it happening again were low, but not zero.

Margie didn't catch her toe on a board or get tangled up in the leash. She could hear the women calling out to each other as they approached the stairs, deciding on a strategy. What would Margie do if she had a three-person team in pursuit of a suspect? Send one in either direction toward the next set of stairs, and the third straight down after her.

The voice that answered them was male. The unknown person in the trees had emerged, and it was a man. Not an old, shaking voice. Younger, Margie's age, perhaps. A much more significant threat to her than either of the women. Margie put on a burst of speed. She needed to get out ahead of him. She needed to reach the next landing before whichever of the women was sent in that direction. To get past it along the shore or escape back up the next set of stairs.

She nearly forgot why she had come down so close to the water and had to stop, looking for a location number. With a sigh of relief, she found a stenciled number and reported it back to the dispatcher. "I am turning right and following the shore to the next landing," she reported.

The dispatcher wanted a compass point. What cardinal direction was Margie was moving? But she had no idea.

"Down the stairs and to the right," she insisted. She looked down at her hands as she turned. Sometimes when she was in a hurry or trying to follow the directions on her GPS, she mixed up right and left. But she was sure she had it correct this time. She was turning right. If the police sent after her went down the stairs and turned right, they would find her.

If they got there in time.

How long could she play cat and mouse with her pursuers?

Three against one. Or three against two, if she counted Stella. She shouldn't count Stella out. She was a sweet dog, but she could still threaten, and had protected Margie from a canine attacker before. Margie could only hope she would react the same way if her attacker were human.

She looked up as she turned to take the goat trail to the right. She could see the man coming down the stairs clearly for a moment before hiding herself in the trees.

She had seen him at the picnic. The grandson or the spouse of one of the granddaughters. She didn't think that it would be a spouse. Why would one of them agree to help Vi or Helen Chang? It had to be Vi's son, Ryan Smith. She reported the names to the dispatcher, thinking that if Ryan or one of the others caught up to her and something happened, at least someone would know who it had been. They would have her own testimony against him.

Stella yipped excitedly. Margie went with her, pressing forward.

She was too close to the water. The goat path was carved into the top of a little embankment, inches from the drop-off that would send her toppling into the water.

She had never learned to swim, too afraid of the water. She had no life jacket on. Only clothes that would weigh her down, growing heavier and dragging her down. And despite what she had thought about fish sunning themselves in the shallows, there was no shallow water. In most places along this side, the sides were steep except in the areas where the water and time had eroded it, creating small shelves here and there. But there were none of these little shores beside Margie now.

Stella barked at Margie, pulling on the leash and tugging her onward. Margie forced herself to move faster. She couldn't let herself think of the water and what would happen if she slipped or lost her balance.

She could hear Ryan behind her, reaching the pathway and crashing through the bush like a buffalo. She slid her phone into her jacket pocket and kept going.

She was a runner. Granted, she had never been particularly fast and she generally stuck to the paved pathways. She had the experience and the stamina. Ryan was a bartender. She was sure he didn't get much exercise. He might have longer legs and more testosterone, but he hadn't trained for this. He was just helping out his mother. And probably regretting it by this time.

Had the whole thing been Vi's idea? Tired of her father's interference in her life, the way that he had controlled her for decades, had she finally broken and decided to take the opportunity of the family gathering to pour him a spiked cocktail and end his reign? She had won her freedom from Scott Smith. Richard's death would give her a cash injection and freedom from her father.

How had she convinced Helen Chang to give her the prescription she needed in someone else's name? It didn't make any sense to her.

Ryan was getting closer.

Margie looked back to measure the distance. Her toe hit a root or a rock in that moment, and she went sprawling.

Except that she didn't land on solid ground. She flew through the air, and the ground slipped out of reach.

She rolled and grabbed and tried to get back there, but before she knew what had happened, she was in the cold water.

CHAPTER TWENTY-TWO

*M*argie closed her mouth and held her breath, swallowing the scream. She went down and down under the water without hitting the bottom. It was colder than anything she could have imagined.

She held her breath but didn't know how long that would work. Would she be like one of those people written up in the scientific journals who survived drowning because of how cold the water was?

Would they take her to the hospital, still not breathing, until, finally warm, she started again and returned to life?

Something clamped around her wrist and pulled her. Margie resisted. Had she fallen within Ryan's reach, and he was about to pull her out just to kill her? Or was there something living in the water, a predator, just waiting for fresh meat? It wasn't like it was Africa or Australia. There were no crocodiles. It was too cold for such creatures to survive. Ogopogo was another story, but she had never heard about a sea monster living in the reservoir. How would it have gotten there, anyway? It was man-made; the reservoir hadn't existed anciently like Loch Ness and Okanagan Lake.

When she was dragged to the surface and was finally able to take a breath into her aching lungs, Margie realized that the sea monster that had saved her was Stella, her trusted companion. Stella paddled frantically in the water while Margie hung on trying to get her bearings.

There were shouts back and forth, Ryan and the two women trying to figure out what to do. Ryan glared at Margie as if she had planned this as a way to get away from him.

He wasn't coming in after her, at least. The cool spring weather and ice-cold water ensured that.

Would he just stand there watching until she drowned? Get a thick tree branch and try to push her under? At least it appeared that he was not carrying a gun and had no way of reaching her from that distance.

But Margie didn't know how long she could hang on. Her body was numb already. Stella was paddling furiously, but she would tire, especially holding up Margie's weight as well as her own. She was trying to swim back to shore, or back to the edge of the water, as there was no shore, but Margie was holding her back. Stella didn't understand the danger the stranger by the water's edge posed.

There were shouts. Other people arriving. Maybe an alarm had been raised that someone had gone into the water. People would gather, and Ryan and his family would not be able to finish the job they had set out to do.

Margie closed her eyes, trying to focus and conserve energy. If other people were there, she would be safe. As long as she got out of the water soon.

It wouldn't be hard for the police to find her now. They would be getting reports of someone in the water, people calling 9-1-1 for water rescue.

People reached over the embankment, arms outstretched, to try to reach Margie and bring her back to solid ground.

They were all out of reach. Stella's doggie paddle was slowing. She was definitely getting tired.

Margie kicked with her feet. She knew the principles of staying afloat. She had learned them in her first aid classes, even if she had never been able to get into the water in swimming classes as a child. She had been taught how moving her arms and legs, leaning back, and staying calm should keep her afloat.

So she tried. If Stella drowned trying to save her, Margie would never forgive herself.

She kept one hand on Stella just in case, kicked her feet, and kept the other arm moving back and forth.

The pressure on Stella eased, and Margie thought she looked grateful. People shouted encouragement. If Margie kept moving, she would generate a little bit of body heat, and sooner or later, Water Rescue would be there to pull her out.

CHAPTER TWENTY-THREE

*M*argie was feeling foggy when a boat pulled up to her, the men in it calling out directions as they got the boat close enough to her to bump her shoulder. Margie tried to grab on to one of the ropes at the side of it, but her hands were numb, and she wasn't sure if she had a good grip on it. The men reached in to grab her and pull her out.

"Get Stella first," Margie told them. "She saved me."

"Stella? Who is Stella?" one of them asked urgently.

"My dog. She's right here."

"We'll get the dog after you. Don't worry."

"You should get her first. I can't swim," Margie tried to explain to them how Stella had pulled her up and kept her afloat and was, therefore, more tired.

Their hands tightened around her and, after a three-count, she was suddenly hauled out of the water and into the boat. It was a shock to suddenly find herself in a different environment. She gasped, the first really free breath she felt like she'd had in a long time, trying so hard to keep the water out of her mouth and nose, trying to conserve the energy it took to stay afloat.

There was another splash and a thump and Stella landed beside her. She instantly squirmed over on top of Margie and started licking her face.

"Stella!" Margie protested.

She heard the tone of the engine change and knew they were getting ready to turn around and return to whatever launch was closest to the waiting EMTs.

"Wait, wait," she told them, trying to keep her brain working to tell them everything she needed to know. "You need to check my pockets. A prescription bottle."

"What medication are you on?" Hands patted her pockets.

"No, not mine. Evidence. If it fell out, you need to find it." She pictured the little orange plastic cup filling up with water and sinking to the bottom of the reservoir. Hopefully, if it had fallen out, it was still floating somewhere nearby and could be retrieved. Hopefully, it hadn't sunk.

The hands stopped on her jacket pocket and pulled out first her cell phone and then the orange bottle.

"Thank goodness," Margie breathed. "Fingerprints."

"Okay, we'll take care of it. You just relax now. We're going to get you warmed up again and checked out."

Margie murmured a response and closed her eyes. Stella snuggled close to her. Someone put a blanket or two over her.

She dozed off until they reached their destination. She didn't know whether it had been two minutes or an hour. She had just been suspended in space, floating there in the boat, not even worried about being on the water. She had always been afraid to go in a boat before, but it wasn't too bad. Definitely better than being in the water.

When they roused her, she was more alert, her brain

starting to kick in a little. She was able to get to her feet with their help to step off the boat and walk up to the ambulance, rather than having to be carried there like a helpless infant.

Lewis was there, smiling and asking her if she was okay. Margie didn't answer his questions about how she was feeling.

"Three people," she told him. "Helen Chang, Violet Smith, and Ryan Smith. You have to have them picked up. They were here. They tried to stop me."

"They threw you in the water?" he asked. "Tried to drown you?"

"Not exactly."

"Let us have a look at her," one of the EMTs told Lewis, pushing him aside. "You can talk later."

Lewis allowed himself to be swept out of the way. Margie saw him reach for his phone.

The EMTs pronounced Margie to be fine after listening to her lungs and getting her story. Margie made them check Stella too, but she didn't appear to have gotten any water in her lungs either. Margie shook her head when they said she should let herself be taken to the hospital.

"You need to be warmed up and monitored. We just need to make sure—"

"No." Margie pulled the warming blanket they had wrapped around her closer. "I don't need to go to the hospital. I'll warm up. It's not that bad. It isn't winter."

"The water is still plenty cold, and you're shivering—"

"Shivering is good," Margie knew her stuff from first aid training and watching plenty of rescue shows on TV. "If I'm shivering," she tried to avoid chattering as she talked to them, "that means I don't have hypothermia."

"You should still be monitored."

"I'll have first responders around me. They'll notice if something is wrong. Lewis, tell them."

"We'll make sure she's okay," Lewis agreed. He smiled down at Margie, sitting at the back of the ambulance. "You're going to need some dry clothes, though."

"I'll go home, then I'll see you back at the office."

"No, you're not driving by yourself. That's a dangerous enough prospect without you being cold and wet. I'll drive you to your house. You can get warm clothes and leave Stella there, and then I'll drive you downtown. We can come back for your car at the end of the day when you're feeling better. Or tomorrow."

"Fine. But Stella is staying with me."

"You don't want to leave her at the house?"

Margie looked at Stella, who had shaken off the water and was now dry and eager for another adventure. "I don't want to leave her alone either. If you have to watch me, then we need to watch her too. I'm not leaving her by herself at the house."

"Okay," Lewis told her, grinning. "We'll just get you changed into something dry."

"Did they find them? All three of them?"

"They will be at the office when we get there, ready and waiting."

"The three of them together," Margie mused, shaking her head. "I never considered a conspiracy."

CHAPTER TWENTY-FOUR

*V*i and Ryan Smith had already been picked up and placed in separate interview rooms awaiting Margie's arrival. Detective Cruz assured Margie that Helen Chang would be there soon. She had been picked up at her office, returning to work as if it were a perfectly normal day. At least Vi and Ryan had been more sensible, heading to the airport.

Margie looked at the monitors for each room, trying to decide who to talk to. Her first instinct had been to try Vi Smith first. It made sense that an older woman would be more vulnerable and easier to get information from. But Ryan was shifting around in his seat and seemed a lot more worried about being in the police station than Vi, who looked perfectly calm. Bored, even.

"I guess I'll try Ryan."

Cruz nodded his agreement. "You want someone in with you? I'm up on the basics of the case, but not as familiar as Detective Jones. Do you want me to get her?"

Margie nodded. "Yeah."

She wondered if Cruz sensed that she didn't want to be

alone in the room with Ryan, even if he was secured to the table. She knew that he wouldn't be able to do anything to her, but she wanted a buffer. Someone else there to see and hear anything he did or said. Someone to play off of and to put Ryan at a bigger disadvantage.

Cruz agreed. It was a few minutes before he returned with Detective Jones, looking all fired up and ready to confront Ryan. She nodded to Margie.

"Ready to do this?"

"I'm ready," Margie agreed.

They gave a quick knock on the door to warn Ryan of their arrival, opened the door, and selected chairs around the table. Close enough to have an intimate conversation with him, but not so close that they were threatening or that he could reach them. She had seen a prisoner give a detective a bloody nose once, head-butting him even though he was chained up. It was best to give prisoners a bit of space.

"Hello, Ryan," Margie greeted. She pushed a damp curl of hair away from her face. "Well, that was a refreshing dip. You should try it sometime."

"You can't even swim!"

"No," Margie agreed. "Never learned."

"I thought all Indians knew how to swim. Didn't you spend every summer at the watering hole?"

Margie raised a brow at him and shook her head in disbelief.

"Why don't you tell us about your grandfather, Ryan? I gather you didn't like him?"

"The old man was a handful, but he didn't bother me," Ryan blustered. "I know none of his children liked him, but it was different being his grandkid. It wasn't like he could tell us what to do. And he didn't usually try."

"So why did you help kill him?"

"I didn't!" He leaned forward, meeting her eyes to

convince her he was telling the truth. "I didn't have anything to do with it. Mom asked me to come with her to the park today. I didn't know anything about it until today. I was shocked! I didn't have any idea what they had done. Whoever would have thought those old ladies would get together and do something like that?"

"Well... why don't you tell me about that? What did your mom say to you? Why did they do it? I understand why she resented your grandfather, and maybe she also wanted her inheritance. But Dr. Chang... I can't understand why she would have anything to do with it. Was she so upset by what he had done to her clients that she would take revenge on him?"

"What he had done to them?" Ryan repeated in a tone of disbelief. "To Mom and her brothers and sister? No, it was nothing to do with them."

"What, then? Why would she be involved in the plot to kill him?"

Ryan looked at Margie for a moment, his eyes wide. She cocked her head and made a small gesture with her hands, inviting him to talk. Giving him an opportunity to tell his story without being tainted by what anyone else would say.

"Because," Ryan said, blinking and leaning forward even more. "She was his mistress!"

All of the air went out of Margie's lungs. She felt flat, unable to breathe. Pieces of the puzzle fell into place. Helen Chang was the only one at the family picnic who was not a blood relative or married to a blood relative. Everyone else there had been family. Margie had puzzled over it. Why invite the family psychiatrist? She hadn't seen any sign that the woman had been there to mediate any arguments. It was possible that she was there as a family friend, but the only one? Why hadn't anyone else been invited? Why was she the only friend there?

"She was his mistress," she repeated. "Brenda said that Richard had affairs."

Ryan nodded. "The old dog. I gather it went on the whole time they were married. He always had other women on the side. And I guess Dr. Chang... for a long time."

"Did everyone know?"

He shrugged. "I don't know that anyone ever said anything about it right out. But I figured it out pretty quickly. She was always his pet. Sitting close to him. Given the first choice or being the first one to dish up, stuff like that. Even when Grandma was alive."

"He invited her to parties while his wife was still alive?"

"I told you he was a dog. Aunt Brenda hated him. Couldn't understand why Evelyn would stay with Grandpa when he disrespected her like that."

"No," Margie shook her head in disbelief. "I'm not sure why she would either."

"They all got together and cooked this up," Ryan said. He held up his hands. "I had nothing to do with it. Didn't have any idea what was going on. They did it right in front of my eyes."

"They *all* got together?" Jones repeated.

Not just *both*, but *all*. Margie flashed to Agatha Christie's *Orient Express* for an instant, where all of the passengers had a hand in the murder. She looked at Ryan, waiting for his answer.

CHAPTER TWENTY-FIVE

*N*ow that everyone knew who Paddy O'Reilly was, Margie had to wait for twenty minutes until he had shaken hands and talked with all the other detectives and Sergeant MacDonald.

Aunt Brenda waited patiently, rolling her eyes at Margie. Paddy was a superstar in their eyes. The old guard. A detective who had worked the hardest cases with no technology. With nothing but shoe leather and a landline. He had worked cases without any DNA, with only the crudest of fingerprint technology, blood typing, and a basic understanding of human nature not informed by the BAU's theories and profiles. And he had closed cases. There had been some cold cases, some that were impossible to solve without modern DNA evidence and genealogy. But the majority of his cases had been closed.

Eventually, Margie and Jones alone remained in the room, Paddy took the seat by his wife, smiling affably, and the door was closed so they could proceed with their interview without interruption.

"Thank you for coming back in," Margie told them. "I

know this must be inconvenient for you. But we really appreciate your help."

The old couple nodded.

Margie looked at Aunt Brenda. She remembered the change she had witnessed, from this pleasant, fragile-looking auntie to the vengeful sister, happy that Richard had finally gotten what he had coming to him.

"We know," she said firmly.

Brenda and Paddy both stared back at her blankly.

"You know what, dear?" Brenda asked eventually.

"We have been talking to Vi and Helen Chang. We know."

There was a long period of silence. Brenda had a mechanical wristwatch, and in the dead silence of the room, Margie could hear it ticking the seconds away.

Brenda leaned back, folding her arms. "So you know."

Paddy looked befuddled. "What are you talking about?"

Margie felt sorry for Paddy. Not just because he had apparently not known anything about the plot, but because he was an old homicide cop who had known nothing about the plot. He had watched everything unfold before him and not known what was going on right in front of his own eyes.

"Your wife conspired with Helen Chang and Violet Smith to murder Richard."

He laughed. A couple of syllables of real, startled, disbelieving laughter. And then he stopped, looking at his wife, waiting for her to laugh or protest. Brenda just looked back at him and said nothing.

"To hear the others tell it, your wife was the… mastermind. Telling them how to do it. How to avoid detection. She knew about poisons and hiding the flavor and the time it would take for it to work. She knew about fingerprints and means and opportunity. She had listened carefully to all of your old stories and formulated a plan."

Paddy stared at Margie, frozen, clearly stunned by this suggestion. There was no glance at Brenda, no "tell" that he had already known this or played a part in it.

"Helen would provide the poison," Margie went on, "a prescription written for an old patient, and Vi would add it to the gin and tonic. Brenda would be nowhere near either one, so her part would remain undetected. Fiona would deliver the drink to Richard without knowing it was poisoned. Richard would die of an apparent heart attack. I assume you were hoping he would fall ill while he was still with the family, so that he could be taken to the hospital and die while in a doctor's care," Margie directed the comment at Brenda. "He would diagnose a heart attack and there would be no autopsy."

She inclined her head in agreement.

"But Richard didn't die until he was out on the water, so there *was* an autopsy, and TCA showed up in his tox screen. And one of the rowing club employees noticed that he seemed unsteady when he took the kayak out."

"It's too bad that it took so long to take effect," Brenda said flatly. "I would have liked to have seen it. As it was, no one actually got to observe. You missed Scott Smith, though," she pointed out, making sure that Margie didn't miss anyone who had been involved in the conspiracy. "I sent him out to make sure that Richard did not come back."

Paddy gawped at his wife, eyes wide. He put his hand on her arm.

"Brenda... please don't say anything else. We need to get you a lawyer. You can't say anything else."

"I don't care. I'm happy to go to prison for it. Though I don't see how anyone could blame me for stamping out such a miserable worm. Richard should have been stopped years ago. If one of us had stepped forward or we had all banded together before Evelyn died… well, maybe we could have saved her from what she had to go through."

"You don't want to go to prison," Paddy told her emphatically. "Brenda, you don't understand what you're doing."

"After forty years with you, you think I don't understand?" Brenda shot back. "You think I couldn't possibly leave you and our home? It will be worth it. I don't regret a thing."

It didn't seem to matter what Paddy said; Brenda seemed to slap him down harder with each answer. He was looking more and more alarmed with each revelation. He looked across the table at Margie, his eyes pleading with her to make the nightmare stop.

But it wasn't going to stop. When word got out that the wife of a former police detective had conspired to murder her former brother-in-law, it was going to make news all around the world.

CHAPTER TWENTY-SIX

*W*hen Margie finally finished interviewing each of the conspirators and seeing them off to booking, she made her way back to her desk.

Her body was sore all over, her muscles aching from the exertion at the park and from the tension she had been holding in her body all day long. She was glad to reach the end of the day and was ready to go home.

Lewis was sitting in her chair. Stella was stretched out comfortably beside him, looking as if she was used to spending her days at the office. Margie laughed.

"The two of you look comfortable."

"I am." Lewis tipped the chair back and stretched. "You have a very comfortable chair, you know. I wouldn't mind spending a bit more time at the desk if I had a chair like this."

Margie knew that time at a desk was the last thing Lewis wanted, so she didn't feel threatened by the suggestion. He would not be looking for a transfer to Margie's team. He wasn't ready to leave undercover behind.

"And you," Margie said to Stella, "You like my office too?"

The dog stretched and yawned. She looked at Margie, tail thumping on the floor.

"Are you ready to go home? To see Christina?"

Stella was on her feet in an instant and gave a little whine.

"Yeah? Okay. Let's get you home. I'm sure Christina will be missing you… Oh!" Margie made a sudden realization, and heat rushed to her cheeks. "I left a note, but I don't know if Christina saw it. I don't want her thinking that Stella is missing!"

Lewis raised one hand to stop her. "I already talked to her."

"You did?"

"She called earlier. I saw her name on the caller ID and didn't think you would mind if she and I chatted. So she's fine. She knows you've got Stella, and I told her we would bring something for dinner, though it might be late."

"You did? You don't think that was a little presumptuous?"

"Well, I am taking you home." He cocked his head. "Right?"

Margie remembered her car was still at Glenmore Park.

"Oh, right. I guess so. We need to go pick the car up."

"Or we can arrange to do that tomorrow. You must be exhausted today."

"Yes, but then I would need to take the bus or Uber to work tomorrow."

"Or I could pick you up."

"What, are you my personal driver now?" Margie teased. "I could get used to this."

"Just until you get your car back. I don't think you need

any extra work tonight. You just cracked a big case. And it was a rather... tiring day."

"You don't know the half of it," Margie admitted, stretching her sore muscles.

They headed for the elevator. "So you want to pick up a pizza on the way home?" Lewis suggested.

"Not pizza. We had pizza last night. How about A&W? We can hit the one on 17th Avenue. Christina likes their veggie burger."

"A&W it is," Lewis agreed. "You can just sit back and relax and not have to do anything else tonight."

Nothing except telling Christina about the day she'd had. It was going to take a little finesse to convince Christina that Margie's life had never been in danger.

But Parks Pat was up for a challenge.

GLENMORE PARK

*T*he Glenmore Dam was built in 1933, creating the Glenmore Reservoir, the source for approximately 40% of Calgary's water supply. The park (split into North Glenmore Park and South Glenmore Park) was developed around the reservoir.

The reservoir itself offers a place for canoeing, kayaking, sailing, and rowing. It is surrounded by extensive multiuse pathways for walking, running, biking, and occasional sightings of bears or cougars.

The author has attended a number of church and family picnics and wiener roasts in Glenmore Park, followed by a game of catch or frisbee, or a walk along the trails.

South Glenmore also boasts a spray park, accessible playground, and bicycle pump track (a bike track with hills and banks where cyclists pump their bodies up and down to propel bikes forward rather than pedaling.)

The park contains much biodiversity, with many species of birds (waterfowl, raptors, and songbirds) and small mammals (squirrels, chipmunks, and rabbits,) and the occasional large mammals (deer) and predators (the aforementioned bears and cougars.)

Did you enjoy this book? Reviews and recommendations are vital to making a book successful.

Please leave a review at your favorite book store or review site and share it with your friends.

Don't miss the following bonus material:
Sign up for mailing list to get a free bonus
Read a sneak preview chapter
Other books by P.D. Workman
Learn more about the author

Get the Parks Pat Survival Pack!

Sign up for my newsletter and receive the **exclusive Parks Pat Survival Pack**, packed with bonus materials and extra goodies you won't find anywhere else.

Stay in the loop on new releases, special offers, and insider content—all delivered straight to your inbox.

Sign up today and start your adventure with Parks Pat!

https://pdworkman.com/the-parks-pat-survival-kit-mystery-police-procedural/

Here's what's inside:
- **Out with the Sunset (Book 1, eBook)**

Begin Margie's journey with her first gripping case as a Calgary homicide officer in the Parks Pat Mysteries.

- **Out with the Sunset (Book 1, Audiobook – Computer Narrated)**

Take the mystery on the go—perfect for your commute, workout, or a walk through the park.

- **Bonus Prequel Story: *Flight of the Bluejay***

Discover Margie's *true beginning*. Before she was a sleuth, she was a pregnant teen on the streets—fighting to survive and find her place in the world.

- **Discover Calgary's Treasures – Photo Minibook**

Step into the beauty of Calgary with this exclusive photo album showcasing the first 15 parks that inspired the series.

- **Digital Wallpapers**

Bring the beauty of Calgary's parks to your phone, tablet, or computer with stunning photography.

SNEAK PEEK AT PERIL IN
THE BLOOMS

CHAPTER ONE

*I*t was a beautiful day. The morning was pleasant, the heat of the day not yet kicking in. Margie was sure that by midafternoon, it would be too hot to spend much time outside, but the ceremonies would be over by then, and she would be back at home or at the air-conditioned office if she decided to go in for the afternoon.

Moushoom, sitting in his wheelchair with a blanket across his lap, would be back to his temperature-controlled bedroom. She was glad that they had decided to go to the reopening of the botanical gardens together. Moushoom always seemed ten times better after spending time outside in the fresh air. Like Antaeus, the Titan in Greek mythology who gained strength from contact with the earth. That was Moushoom, gathering strength when he was in contact with nature. He remembered all the old stories, all that he had learned at the sides of his parents and grandparents back before modern technology.

When she had heard about the opening of the newly refreshed gardens at Riley Park, she hadn't thought much of it initially. What she remembered of Riley Park from when she was a child visiting Calgary was the wading pool.

Until then, a "wading pool" had meant that little round, blow-up kiddie pool that her family had filled with the garden hose. Too cold to put her feet into when it was first filled up, and then warming in the sun. The pristine water getting clouded with leaves and grass clippings and bugs as she and her cousins hopped in and out of it throughout the day.

The wading pool at Riley Park was something different altogether. It was a vast concrete structure, constantly filtered and refilled like a swimming pool, with all those curves and dips and hills, filled with laughing, shrieking children and lounging adults trying to escape the heat. It had seemed enormous to her at the time, and she wondered whether her memory was accurate.

Back then, she hadn't even been aware of any gardens. There had been a small playground with a swing set, slide, and rusting animal shapes mounted on springs. There were huge trees and a lone squirrel that ran along the telephone wires back before the gray squirrel population in Calgary had exploded and squirrels were everywhere. She didn't remember any gardens.

Now there was a large, colorful playground full of climbing equipment, slides, and a saucer swing. And there was an adult playground with parallel bars, a climbing net, and various other equipment that Margie would have to read the instructions to know how to use.

"We used to come here to watch cricket," Moushoom told her as she pushed his wheelchair along the pathway. Margie had been staring at the different varieties of trees, trying to identify each one. She had no idea what most of them were. She identified an oak tree by the wavy shape of its leaves. And a maple. But most of them, she was clueless about. One of them was full of red fruit that looked like cherries. Did cherries grow in Alberta? Big ones like that, not the little chokecherries she was familiar with?

Stella strained on the leash, wanting to go everywhere, to smell everything. There was a whole world of sights and scents that needed to be cataloged.

"Cricket?" Margie repeated, wondering if Moushoom was feeling all right. Who would watch cricket in Calgary? She wondered whether he meant a different sport, or if he had been watching cricket on TV at the home and was confusing it with reality.

"Yes. Big cricket pitch over there," Moushoom waved with one hand.

"Oh, is there?"

There was a large green field. Margie supposed it could have been used for cricket or soccer. But there were no stands. No soccer goalposts. She couldn't see any field of play marked out in the grass.

They made their way around the trees on the paved pathway, and the wading pool came into view. It was huge, with curves sprawling across the park. There was a splash park that hadn't been there when she was a child. At least, not that she could remember. She was glad the wading pool really was big, and that it hadn't just been a childhood memory with everything out of scale.

"Wow, look at it. I can't believe how big it is."

"We brought so many grandchildren and cousins to this pool," Moushoom remembered. "They always had a great time."

"Unless there were wasps," Margie recalled. "I remember one year there was a huge number of wasps. They were everywhere."

"Did you get stung?"

"No."

It was funny that the wading pool had not triggered Margie's fear of the water. But then, it wasn't more than two feet deep anywhere. She didn't have to worry about drowning in it, about not being able to touch the bottom, the water closing over her head. It had been a fun, safe place to play, no more dangerous than the bathtub.

The pathway wound around the pool to the other side, where Margie saw a clubhouse of some kind.

"Cricket," Moushoom repeated.

Margie pushed the wheelchair around the building.

CALGARY & DISTRICT
  CRICKET LEAGUE
  (1908)

Margie laughed. "Cricket," she agreed. "Did you like the games? Were they fun to watch?"

He nodded. "Some of those bowlers… you wouldn't believe how fast they can throw."

Margie could see someone practicing, throwing ball after ball. She wouldn't have wanted to be in the path of that cannon.

"It looks like the opening is happening over here," she motioned to a flat area where folding chairs had been set up. There was a podium at the front and a few men were setting up speakers.

"Push me right up to the front," Moushoom instructed. "I want to be able to see everything."

"Okay," Margie laughed and agreed. There would be no sitting in the back and staying anonymous today.

CHAPTER TWO

ents and shades had been set up around the gardens to keep them out of sight until the big reveal. But other smaller gardens were already visible. They were filled with a riot of color, orange and red and purple and yellow. Margie stopped beside one to take in the individual flowers and watch the bees buzzing around them.

"These are amazing," she said. "Look at all of the different kinds of flowers."

"Some of these were in my kokum's garden," Moushoom told her, speaking of his own grandmother. Margie's great-great-grandmother. Margie had only seen pictures of her; they had never met. Moushoom's mother had been alive when Margie was born, but had died soon after. Margie had no recollection of her either. She only came alive in Moushoom's stories.

"She knew her medicine," Moushoom told Margie. "She always had just the herbs the family needed close at hand. And enough for friends and neighbors, too. She took care of people."

"How did she know how to use them? From her mother?"

"Many generations of mothers," Moushoom agreed. "All of the stories and herblore passed down through the generations. There was no pharmacy to run to then, only to Mother Earth. She taught us what we needed to know."

Margie maneuvered Moushoom's wheelchair across the grass. It was a lot more difficult than using the paved pathway, but she didn't have far to go.

"Can I put my grandfather here?" she asked a pinch-faced middle-aged woman who was giving the sound men directions.

The woman looked at her, frowning, and then around the chairs that had been set up. "Didn't anyone leave space for wheelchairs?" she demanded.

The other busy employees in matching blue t-shirts looked around at each other, shaking heads.

"Oh, good grief." The woman marched over and pulled a chair out of line at either end of the front two rows to make space for wheelchair seating. "Please. If that isn't enough space, take another one out," she told Margie.

Margie nodded her thanks and pushed Moushoom's wheelchair into place. She tied Stella's leash to the arm of the wheelchair. The woman gave more instructions to the various employees working on getting everything set up. They seemed to be running a little late, as people were already gathering and talking.

The woman finished and approached Margie. She looked at Moushoom in the wheelchair.

"Is this one of our special guests?" she asked. "I am Dr. Eliza Thorndyke." She offered a dry, thin hand for each of them to shake.

"No, we just came for the opening," Margie told her. "It looked interesting and it's been forever since I have been to

Riley Park, so we thought we would come along and have a look."

"Well, welcome, I'm glad you could make it." Her eyes kept returning to Moushoom. "We have a land acknowledgment at the beginning of the ceremony. I would like to make sure that your people are mentioned. What tribe…?"

"We are Métis," Margie said, her cheeks warming. This was not territory she had navigated often.

"We acknowledge Treaty 7. Are you included in Treaty 7?"

"No," Moushoom said strongly. "We did not sign the Treaty."

Thorndyke nodded. "Right, of course. I should know that, I'm sure. Should I just include… the Métis people, or is there a specific organization…?"

"We are Métis," Moushoom said. "We don't need a number."

Margie was aware that Calgary fell into District 5 and 6, but she didn't know which Riley Park was in. Besides, the districts were not the way the Métis identified. They were simply for governance.

"I'll be sure to include you in the land acknowledgment," Thorndyke said. She scurried to the podium and flipped through pages, a pen held in one hand as she scowled down at what was written and scratched in some changes. Margie looked at Moushoom, and he shrugged. It was weird how these land acknowledgments had become a thing at every public event. Margie wasn't sure how she felt about them or if they had any real meaning.

After a few minutes, as the speakers for the opening sat down in a row behind the podium, Thorndyke leaned in to the microphone and tapped it, creating a noise on the speakers that made everyone jump, and several cover their ears.

"Could everyone take their seats?" Thorndyke suggested, satisfied that the sound system was working. "We will get started shortly."

The audience chairs started to fill. It was easy to see that they had not anticipated such a large gathering. There were few empty chairs, and a number of people stood in the back or around the sides to watch.

Thorndyke looked at her watch and began, speaking too close to the microphone and again blasting everyone's eardrums.

"I am gratified to see so many people here today who are interested in preserving and expanding the gardens. These plants and flowers do more than just provide the eye with beauty. They are vital to the health of the environment and to us individually."

She paused to give them all a big smile. It looked forced. It looked like it was something she had been coached to do rather than being normal and natural. Margie suspected it was written into her script: STOP AND SMILE.

"We acknowledge that we are on Treaty 7 territory and the traditional land of the Métis people. We acknowledge and respect the histories, languages, and diverse cultures of the First Nations who traditionally live, work, and play on this land."

Another pause and smile.

There was a sharp report that made Margie first tense in her seat, looking around, and then jump to her feet. She looked at Dr. Thorndyke, who was looking startled and confused. Margie could just see the pant leg of her tan pants around the podium, suddenly stained red at the thigh.

Margie turned around, scanning the throng behind her, who at first were frozen in place, and then dissolved into chaos. A figure wearing a ball cap and hoodie broke into a run, heading away from the crowd and toward the edge of the park. Margie sprinted after him.

It was a few long seconds before the crowd started to clue in to what had just happened and started making noise. There were some screams and cries of distress, but no more gunshots. Margie had made a split-second decision to pursue the fleeing man rather than staying behind to look for any more attackers or provide first aid to Dr. Thorndyke. There were a lot of people present. Someone else would have first aid knowledge. They would all have cell phones and could call 9-1-1. The fact the man was running away meant that he was probably alone and no further violence was intended. The biggest risk was losing him because she had not acted quickly enough.

Margie had started running in the mornings before work, when she could get herself up early enough. But jogging, not sprinting. Good for cardio, good to get the blood flowing and get some benefit from it—but she had never been fast, even in foot races as a child. Certainly not now, putting in too much time behind a desk and eating too much fast food and pasta.

She kept the man in view as long as she could, cataloging every detail she could. Height. Build. Coloring. What he was wearing from head to foot. He wasn't carrying anything. She couldn't tell whether he still had the gun or not, and Margie didn't have hers. She was off duty, on an outing with her grandfather to look at the gardens; of course she wasn't armed. It was Canada.

The whole thing was over in a couple of minutes. The man made it out of the park and across the street, and Margie was trailing behind him, too slow, losing him in the traffic and between the parked cars. He might have made it into one of the buildings; she hadn't seen. But she had lost him.

She stopped running and pulled out her phone, dialing 9-1-1. She hoped everybody at the park hadn't called at once and overwhelmed the dispatchers.

"This is Detective Patenaude," she identified herself quickly once she reached the emergency operator. "I was at Riley Park at the shooting. Pursued the shooter but lost him. I am at…" Margie looked at the street signs and read them off to the dispatcher. "He is on foot in this area, within a block or two. If you can get a perimeter up fast enough, you might still be able to catch him. Suspect is wearing a black hoodie, Flames ball cap, blue jeans, white sneakers. The hood was pulled up over his head, but he might have removed it to change his appearance after getting out of my sight."

She stopped for a moment to catch her breath and let the dispatcher get all of that down and start dispatching units. "I did not get a good look at the suspect's face, but he appeared to be a slimly built male, light-skinned, around six feet tall. May still be armed. He's been running, so he may be out of breath. He was fast." She blew out her breath again, wishing she had been able to catch him or get a better description.

"Stay where you are, detective," the dispatcher told her. "A unit will come to talk to you, so you can give him more information about the suspect's speed and direction."

Margie had turned around to return to the park, but she stopped and stayed where she was. It would only be a minute or two before the car got to her, and maybe they could catch the shooter before he got away.

She took deep breaths. Her chest was burning. It had been a much harder run than what she was used to.

Peril in the Blooms, Book #15 of the *Parks Pat Mysteries*
series by P.D. Workman
can be purchased at pdworkman.com or at your favorite
online retailer

ABOUT THE AUTHOR

P.D. Workman is a USA Today Bestselling author and multi-award winner, renowned for her prolific output of over 100 published works that span various genres. With a knack for crafting page-turners, Workman captivates readers with everything from cozy mysteries like the Auntie Clem's Bakery series to gripping young adult and suspense novels.

A prolific reader and writer since childhood, P.D. Workman crafts emotionally powerful stories that don't shy away from hard topics. Her books tackle mental illness, addiction, abuse, and trauma with raw honesty and compassion, giving voice to the often unheard. If you crave authentic, character-driven page-turners that hit deep and stay with you long after the final page, you're in the right place.

With each new release, fans eagerly anticipate another thrilling blend of thought-provoking storytelling and relatable characters that define P.D. Workman's brand as an author of unforgettable page-turners—gripping tales that leave a lasting impact long after the last page is turned.

P. D. Workman, does not shy from probing the deep psychological scars of childhood trauma, mental illness, and addiction. Also characteristic of this author, these extremely sensitive issues are explored with extensive empathy, described with incredible clarity, and portrayed with profound insight.

Some of Workman's titles have been translated into Spanish, French, Portuguese, German, and Italian.

Workman began writing at an early age and is a prolific reader as well as writer. She is also passionate about teaching and learning, expresses her creativity through art and cooking, and loves exploring the Calgary parks and green spaces where the Parks Pat Mysteries are set. She was a legal assistant for many years and has done extensive charitable work.

Workman was born and raised in Alberta, Canada, and is married with one adult son.

Please visit P.D. Workman at pdworkman.com to see what else she is working on, to join her mailing list, and to link to her social networks.

If you enjoyed this book, please take the time to recommend it to other purchasers with a review or star rating and share it with your friends!

tiktok.com/@pdworkmanauthor

facebook.com/pdworkmanauthor

x.com/pdworkmanauthor

instagram.com/pdworkmanauthor

amazon.com/author/pdworkman

bookbub.com/authors/p-d-workman

goodreads.com/pdworkman

linkedin.com/in/pdworkman

pinterest.com/pdworkmanauthor

youtube.com/pdworkman

Find P.D. Workman's books at

PDWORKMAN.COM

Scan the QR code below

www.ingramcontent.com/pod-product-compliance
Lightning Source LLC
Chambersburg PA
CBHW020615250626
47154CB00004B/1519